The 25th Demon

A fictional psychological thriller.
Third Edition

By Dr. JParker Griffin, Jr.

ii

Table of Contents

The 25th Demon

CHAPTER 1—The Discard

Standing on the edge of the terrace, a breeze ruffles through a handsome, medium build, 5 ft. 11-inch-tall man's silky and expensive sprayed hair. He looks down and sees as people are gathered around the rooftop pool area enjoying themselves, surrounded with fresh greenery, exotic palm trees. Radiant party lights strung throughout the area making the pool's water look like crystalline diamonds. Lavish Ceramic flower pots filled with large-bloom petunias line the perimeter of the pool deck. As he further checks out the view, he sees the beautiful city skyline twinkling just like the stars were shining in the night sky. People are dancing, laughing, socializing and living their best lives, sipping cocktails and devouring hors d'oeurves.

The handsome man standing on the terrace was also tapping his foot to the beats of international deep house music from New York, London, Chicago, and Paris. People are swimming in the pool in celebration of fashion week, wearing lavish swimsuits. A buffet of delicate finger sandwiches, carved roast beef, Alfredo pasta, and exquisitely prepared salads was being served as people watched with fascination, magicians executing magic and card tricks.

As the handsome man moves away from the edge of the terrace he stops and looks himself in the mirror at the end of the terrace, admiring his $8,500 designer suite with an open shirt collar. Smirking to himself he slips away to a private area of the terrace. He stands with his back on the waist-height glass rail to a staircase leading down to the next lower floor. His face concealed by the darkness of the secluded area was not visible to anyone, only the silhouettes of his body were apparent. He recognizes a brown-haired beauty dressed in a short black dress, dripping in diamond jewelry and gold accessories, walking towards him. The man irritated by her presence asks snappily, "Okay Monica, I'm here. What do you want?"

The brown-haired woman anxiously speaks, "PD, listen! I have to tell you some..." PD cuts her sentence already annoyed, "What the hell do you think I'm here for? Spit it out! Without missing a beat Monica replies, "I'm pregnant!"

Upon hearing this news PD's eyes widen and he becomes even more angry, "You're what? Pregnant? How's that my problem? I told you to use protection!" Monica in confusion and anger, points a finger at PD's face, "It's going to be your problem when you're paying child support! $29 hundred a month. Child support or jail, you decide! Imagine your pretty little wimp ass being somebody's bitch in there! Coward!"

PD walks toward her slowly, talking in a calm and stern tone, "It's not mine. Prove it!" Monica narrowing her mascara layered eyes, smiles sarcastically, "Ha, everybody knows about us. I've got all the proof I need, asshole. Semen, hair, even a little blood from your shaver."

Cutting her sentence, PD continues, "Bullshit! Paternity test I presume? You're going to get an abortion, or I'm going to kick your ass! I ought to throw your pale ass down those steps right now!"

Smirking, Monica says, "Oh PD, I wish you would put your hands on me!

PD chuckles evilly, "Really? Your slut ass can't prove shit!" He smirks and begins to walk away.

Monica furiously calls out to him, "Huh? I can't huh? Go ahead. Walk away like a little punk ass little boy. You couldn't be a father anyway. Because you couldn't ever be a man! The sex wasn't shit. You're not shit! Pencil dick!

PD stops in his tracks upon hearing all these insults, his eyes bulge out in rage. His face is contorted with anger, and he crimps the corner of his mouth gritting his teeth. He spins around and runs toward her grabbing her tightly around the neck shaking and choking her forcefully, "What did you say? Not what! Don't you ever. . . bitch!"

Monica struggling under his strength scratching his hands off her neck, "You're not! You'll never be! Get your hands off me, little boy! Let go! Let go of me! I'll scream!" Shaking with rage PD put more pressure into choking her, "Open your big fucking mouth, and I'll throw your ass over this rail!"

Monica fights for her life, slapping and kicking him. As she begins to scream PD covers her mouth and lifts her up on the rail as they struggle with each other. PD threatens her, "Say one more word, and I swear I'll drop your ass over this ledge!"

Monica's eyes are bulging out with fear and slowly slipping over the ledge. She tries to grab his jacket with his name sewn in and tears off one of the hand-made buttons from his expensive tailor-made designer suit, "Help! Help!" He tries to save her to keep her from falling by grabbing her arm but she slowly slips out of his grasp. The ground rapidly spins up toward her as she is falling while flailing her arms and legs in order to hold onto something, anything but in vain. PD thinks, *Oops! Faggot bitch!* He looks over the edge of the building and sees her lying on the ground in a puddle of blood, groaning and barely alive like a broken rag doll.

CHAPTER 2—Lost Love, Lost Innocence

In front of the luxury condominium, a T.V. entertainment commentator is shooting a video for Fashion Week, "We're here in the heart of Fashion Week." His sentence is cut off by a blood-curdling scream. Everyone seems in utter shock as the woman is falling from the roof. The young lady's body is pierced by one of the steel vertical poles that supports the video background screen where they are filming the proposed interviews. Blood covers the background screen and splashes slightly on the commentator and the crowd. The crowd gasps and looks up to the top of the building and see a medium build white male looking down at them. In fear of getting caught, he runs off. The commentator shouts in panic, "Somebody call 911! Call 911!"

Half an hour later, barging through the crowd is the police department detective. The crowd is surrounding the body, still in shock and panic, with wide eyes. Detective Cuffie making his way through the crowd, showing his badge, "Excuse me. Excuse me. Please let me through. Detective Anthony Cuffie, police department. Official police business."

Detective Cuffie presses his way to the front of the crowd and sees that the rooftop girl impaled on the steel rod is his goddaughter, Monica.
His face becomes pale suddenly as all the blood drained out of his face, "Oh, no. Hell no. Monica!!! No Monica!" Still shocked detective Cuffie sees that Monica is tightly grasping the hand-made tailored button from a jacket. Dazed, Detective Cuffie walks twenty feet or so away from the scene of the accident and recalls his goddaughter, Monica's words. People are laughing and socializing in the background. Detective Cuffie and Monica are having a private conversation in the living room of Monica's house.

Monica barely containing her excitement says, "Dad, I've finally done it." Detective Cuffie confused as to what she's referring to, asks, "Done what?" Not beating around the bush anymore Monica tells, "I found my soulmate! He's like no one I've ever met or known. Wait until you see him. I think I'm in love! Detective Cuffie happy for his goddaughter exclaims with adoration in his eyes, "Great!"

Coming back to reality Detective Cuffie stares off into the darkness and thinks to himself, *God as my witness. I'm going to find whoever killed Monica. He's going under the jail. Trust me!*

A bystander comes to Detective Cuffie and says, "Detective, I saw some guy looking over the edge of the building where she fell from. I think I've seen him before." The detective totally shattered by the chain of events says, "She was my goddaughter"
The bystander, gazing with a look of pity on his face replies, "Sorry to hear that. Didn't look like an accident to me. Here's my name and phone number just in case."

A stale smell permeates the house. Everything is covered in dust and dirt. Dirty laundry and half eaten meals are on the floor. An eight-year-old child remembers as he cries and ravenously finishes a stale sandwich. He recalls the sinister way that Uncle Mason and his brother, Martin, locked him in a cold, dark closet over the weekend. Young PD suddenly freezes with fear as the door closes loudly and a large burly man with red eyes and foul-smelling breath comes closer, puts his hands over his ears, shouts at the child, "Shut up!" The child whimpers in terror and says, "I didn't do anything." The man becomes more furious, "PD, didn't I tell you to shut up! I'm tired of your whimpering ass! Do you want to spend another day in there?", he says pointing toward the closet.

Young PD shivering with fear repeats himself, "Martin, I didn't do anything."
Martin no longer containing his anger, bursts out, "I said shut up, PD! Get your ass out of there. Come here! As Young PD takes small, fearful steps forcefully towards Martin, he grabs him by his hair and repeatedly swings the stinging small plastic baseball bat and hits Young PD across his back, head and

shoulders. Martin's mind's eye sees images of lust as
he forcefully removes PD's clothes. PD struggles to get
out of his clutches, "Let go of me, Martin! Leave me
alone. Help! I'm going to tell daddy! Martin stops and
laughs sarcastically, "What daddy? Your mom and
dad doesn't want you. Why do you think she sent you
here and he left you? Huh?" PD crying hysterically
says, "I'm going to find him, and you're going to be
sorry about the way you treated me. You're an
asshole!"

Martin smirks and licks his lips again, "In the
meantime, take this!" Martin pounds the plastic bat
on PD's back again. He forcefully pushes him on the
small cot where he monstrously rapes Young PD and
leaves when he's done, zipping his jeans, banging the
door closed. Young PD whimpers lying on a filthy cot
covered with blood and a dirty, grey blanket, in a fetal
position staring off in a distance as he's mentally
traumatized.

CHAPTER 3—Lovebombing

PD is running on the treadmill and checking out the crisp and clean environment of the health spa and fitness club that he visits often. As he's running his eyes around the gym, he spots an attractive female power walking on the treadmill beside him.

PD suddenly decides to strike up a conversation, "Hello, angel! How are you doing?"

The woman upon hearing him removes her earphones, looks towards him and smiles, "Fine, and you? What's your name?"

PD smirks, "Purvis Dempsey, but they call me "PD". And you?"The woman attracted by PD's confidence, replies, "Kara, Kara Taylor." They both get off the treadmill to catch their breath. Self-conscious about her looks, Kara checks herself out in the mirror. PD notices it and boastfully thinks to himself, *Of course. I'm a masterpiece!*

Getting back to the conversation PD asks, "Have I seen you before? Work out here a lot? PD exhibits his trademark sniffle, Kara doesn't take much notice of it.

"I've been working out here for months. I need to get back into working out more often", Kara replies.

PD seizing the opportunity, flirts with her, "I see, I need to work out here more often if you're going to be here." Giving his trademark full teeth smile women and even men die over, he asks "What do you do?" Kara obviously caught under his spell replies, "I'm in information tech, but I mostly work in the fashion industry." "Fashion?" PD sniffles again, "You're kidding!"

Kara finally notices his sniffles, "No, seriously. Do you have a cold?" She peers into PD's captivating eyes as if she is hypnotized. She is instantly infatuated with PD but cleverly conceals her intense feelings for him. PD replies, "Pollen. It's getting the best of me." changing the topic he asks, "Where do you work?" "Pinnacle Designs", she says, "I'm the V.P. of creative designs. It's a big title, mostly for show, but I'm happy to have it!", Kara replies confidently.

PD further executing his suave womanizing moves with laser precision, says, "Let's get to know each other better. Join me for a snack? I got a taste for fried chicken and pork chops." Kara didn't waste a second and accepted the offer, "Okay. I'd like that!"

Kara is lying on her stomach, on her bed, smiling and recalling these past six weeks where PD showered his love-bombing moves on her by taking her to various dates around town. That included kite flying, driving high speed motorized go carts with her, you name it. With a chain of amazing rendezvous behind them, they also enjoyed New York City's club scene where they both dressed impeccably and competed with each other in a house music club dance contest. PD faced Kara and they showed off their Brooklyn-honed Loose Legs dance skills. (Loose Legs is an urban dance that many hip people in the New York and around the world do. Check it out on the Internet.)

For good measure, PD continued to groom Kara by showing her his soft, compassionate side. He took her to a dog pound where PD surprised her with a white furry puppy with a name tag around its neck, reading, "Fluffy". Kara remembered all of it with a wide love-struck smile, thinking to herself, *I'm lucky to have this man!*

As she became lost in her thoughts, she heard her phone ring. *Oh, it must be PD.* She sees the caller ID and it's definitely him. Smiling, she answers the call, "Hello PD, I was just thinking about you!" PD, "Hey Kara. Drop by my apartment next week. I'll have some snacks. We'll have fun. Okay?" Kara, not missing a beat, accepted the offer, "Okay. Guacamole and chips?" PD replies, "Got it. See you next week", and hung up the phone.

PD is in his lavish condo, snorting a line of cocaine in his bedroom. He steps out of the bedroom to the living room where he is practicing his house music dance moves by watching an online house music dance class from Jardi Santiago. The dancers on the computer screen perform house music club steps from worldwide; places like Massachusetts, California, Germany, Singapore, Florida, Ohio, Malaysia, Belgium, and Australia. He performs an outstanding house music dance routine. As he finishes dancing, the doorbell rings. PD pauses the video and goes to check out who's at the door.

He opens the door and Kara steps in, "Hey PD." "Hey angel" PD replies and embraces Kara. After closing the door PD asks, "Do you want the Guacamole and chips you asked for?" "Oh, sure" Kara replies. She thinks *PD has been so good to me. I'm gonna give'em some. He's going to get a surpri . . . . under this dress.* As Kara is smiling to herself, drunk with PD's charisma, PD notices and asks, "Hey what are you thinking about?" "Oh, you'll see", Kara replies while smirking.

PD brings the food to Kara and turns on slow music to set the mood. As they finish the food, PD asks Kara to dance with him. As they dance to some slow, sensual music, Kara places her arms around PD's neck. PD has his face buried in Kara's neck, giving her soft kisses, his one hand on his waist and other is sensually and slowly moving towards her behind.

Kara looks into PD's eyes and leans closer for a kiss. Their lips barely touching, then holding her face, PD takes charge and kisses her passionately while caressing her luscious behind with the other hand. Kara moans as PD continues to kiss her using his tongue this time. They break off to take a breath and PD takes her to his bedroom.

As PD notices Kara's lips swollen from kissing, his dick begins to get hard. He orders Kara to take off her dress. As she gradually takes off her dress, PD is getting more and more turned on. His hardness is visible through his sweat pants as he undresses too. Kara reveals a sexy red lacy bra and panty, which was hardly hiding anything, and she takes off her dress completely. Her hard, pink nipples are clearly visible.

PD bites his lip upon seeing her. He lies her down on the bed and starts kissing her vigorously again. This time he's rubbing his thumbs on her hard nipples. Wanting more, he starts licking her erect nipple while caressing the other. Kara is moaning and moving her hips towards PD. He moves his hand in her panty and starts rubbing her and then fingers her. Kara, moaning loudly, now barely containing her excitement, her heart starts to pound. "Shush, keep quiet!" PD says. PD finally decides to thrust his manhood into Kara, and they move in fast rhythm. Kara moves her hips towards PD as she repeatedly reaches orgasm and moans each time uncontrollably. PD once again admonishes her, "Keep quiet! Real quiet! Concentrate, Kara! Fuck me!" "Quiet? But that takes all the fun out of it" Kara complains. "Shush, . . . just . . . nothing!" PD replies, as they both climax together.

PD briefly escapes into his dream world after having an ecstatic orgasm with Kara. While he's daydreaming, he has a blank look on his face. Kara, lying beside him on the bed, notices this and tries to get his attention, "PD, PD!". . . "Hello!" . . . "Earth to PD."

She gets frustrated and starts moving her hand in front of PD's face, "Are you there?" PD finally snaps back to reality, "Oh. Sorry! I was just thinking about visiting my grandmother in the old folk's home where she stays. Grandma loves me!" Suddenly PD's face lights up and he asks, "Come with me to visit Grandma Dempsey?" Kara obviously touched by the gesture accepts his offer, "Of course PD, I'd love to"

CHAPTER 4—Managing Expectations

Stepping out of the car, Kara and PD make their way towards Perkin's Nursing Home to visit PD's grandmother. They are walking towards the nursing home's door holding each other's hands. They meet up with Grandma Dempsey after being guided by a nurse towards grandma's room. After entering the room Kara sees that an old woman is sitting by the window, deep in thought—grandma. PD decides to kiss his grandma on the forehead and surprises her with his unexpected visit. PD, "Hello grandma. How are you?" Grandma Dempsey looks back and gives PD a huge smile, "Oh PD! I'm fine child. I haven't seen you since. . . forever!" "Yes grandma, work doesn't let me breathe. Anyhow, meet Kara, this is my girlfriend", PD replies. Grandma says, "Girlfriend. You like girls. Hmmm." PD ignores her statement and takes Kara's hand and pulls her in front of him. Kara goes and hugs grandma Dempsey, "Hello, I've heard a lot about you", she says with a smile. Grandma Dempsey likes

Kara a lot; so she says, "Oh, you're beautiful dear. Will you both play checkers with me?" Kara embarrassed by her compliment, blushes and replies, "Oh thank you. And of course, we'll play. Right PD?" "Yes, sure", PD says and takes out the board game out of the cupboard. He sets the board game on the bed.

They smile as they play checkers with grandma Dempsey. Then Kara softly brushes PD's grandmother's hair with great pleasure. PD kisses his grandma on the cheek. They all smile.

A group of young professional singles are running and playing on the beach. PD and Kara are lying under a large beach umbrella and tarp. They are enjoying the ocean breeze when they see a Frisbee fly in front of the two of them where they are lying on their beach blanket. The Frisbee thrower is a rugged, exceptionally handsome young man with a perfect athletic body. He stumbles and falls right in front of PD and Kara.

Kara startled by his fall, asks, "Are you okay, sir?" The young man replies while getting up, a little out of breath, "Oh, sure. I'm okay. Not to worry. At least I retrieved it without breaking my neck", the young man says. As he gets up he notices the woman in front of him and says, "Hey, don't I know you? Kara? What the hell are you doing here? It's Adam, girl." Kara surprised by his presence, "Adam! it's you. Wow! I can't believe it." Adam, flexing his muscles unconsciously, replies, "What in the world are you doing here? What's up gorgeous?" "Oh. My boyfriend and I are just here for a long weekend", she says. Suddenly realizing she didn't introduce PD to Adam, Kara says, "Oh, yes. This is my boyfriend, PD." "Hello, PD. How are you, Sir? It's a pleasure to make your acquaintance", Adam says cordially.

PD replies flirtatiously, "Well, hello there, Sir. The pleasure is _all_ mine!" While eyeballing Adam's outstanding physique very closely, PD asks, "Would you like to join us?"

Kara quickly pitching in, "Oh yes, would you like to have a frozen daiquiri or something?" "Oh no. I have to get going. Anyway, I couldn't intrude", Adam says apologetically. "Oh, think nothing of it", PD replies. "Yeah, no problem", Kara says.

Adam politely refuses, "Oh. Thanks, but I really must get back to my friends." "Okay, Adam. Let's have lunch again some time", Kara offers. Adam accepts the offer, "Sure, no problem. Hit me up next week. It was nice meeting you, PD".

"It sure was nice meeting you, Adam." PD replies eyeing Adam again. Kara says bye to Adam while smiling, "See you Adam." Adam throws the Frisbee, and runs off to rejoin his friends.

PD looks at Kara and says, "Baby, you sure do look great today, as always. You know, I don't remember ever having a woman as awesome as you come into my life. Why are you so drawn to me, baby? Is it because I'm smarter, more attractive, and more savvy than all of these half-baked, run-of-the-mill dudes in this town put together? Wait. I know. It's my self-confidence." PD smirks in a conceited manner. Kara raises her eyebrows, uncontrollably intrigued by his overconfidence and replies sarcastically, "PD, yes, you are the most handsome, classy, and self-confident man that I have ever seen here. You are the perfect gentleman, the perfect mate, the perfect everything. You know I love you." PD laughs pompously, "Now! Take that! That's just what I thought. You're right! I'm God-like!"

PD's eyes are gleaming at her remarks as if intoxicated with Kara's flattery, "You complete me, Kara! You're like a soulmate to me or something like that. I love you, girl." He kisses her all over her face. Kara surprised by PD's sudden profession of love says, "Soulmate? You love me? That's the first time you ever said that!" "Yeah. "Love". It's a special kind of love, conditional." PD replies. Kara is confused by the word PD used, "Conditional? What does that mean?" PD replies, explaining to her, "It means you make me feel like a real man, inside. All warm and mushy. I love myself through you. It's conditional though."

Kara still confused, decides to let it go and changes the topic, "PD, you know what? You know the volunteer work that I do with the shelter—the children's shelter? It really hurts me to my heart to see them suffer the way that they do." PD is deeply engrossed in reading his text messages instead of paying attention to Kara's comments. Kara noticing this tries to get PD's attention, "PD. PD. PD! Are you listening to me? PD". Glaring at Kara with a look of utter evil in his eyes, he replies rudely, "What? Are you some kind of psycho? Don't you see that I'm trying to get something done here?" Kara, hurt and surprised by the sudden change of mood by PD, flies off the handle, "Well, you know what? If that's the way you feel about it, you can kiss my ass!" She throws a pebble at PD really hard which hits him in the forehead. Then she kicks sand at him in frustration. PD furiously shouts, "Damn it, Kara. You ought to be glad that I am who I am."

Kara not taking any of his shit, replies, " Yeah, right. . . a big, sorry ass punk? How dare you call me a psycho? You can take your pitiful-ass self and go to hell!" Kara throws a small piece of driftwood that she had been toying with at PD and storms off to their hotel room. She is sobbing as she mumbles to herself, "I'll see you later in the hotel room. You're an asshole. Now I see why your own mother calls you an asshole! You deserve it!" Kara briskly walks off to their room. PD not affected on the outside, but seething inside, by her behavior continues to fixate on his phone as a message rings on it, "Go ahead on, you, sorry bitch". *That bitch is so sensitive,* PD thought.

He returns to reading the text messages on his phone. He looks at the screen on his cell phone and reads a message, ostensibly from a man, "It's Theo: *Baby, how's the beach? I can't wait to see you, you, sexy bastard."* PD's eyes gleam with excitement as he finishes reading the message.

CHAPTER 5—The Crawl

PD's lounging around half naked in his new apartment, three weeks after the Puerto Rico trip, paid for by Kara. Killer, PD's dog, is running around the apartment doing side-flips, trying to get PDs attention. PD calls Killer, "Hey Killer. Come here, boy!" PD plays vigorously with Killer and softly pets Killer while talking on the phone with Kara. "Hey Kara, thanks for hooking me up with the new apartment condo. I'm going to invite you over for drinks. The apartment is already a design masterpiece. Are you sure you don't mind paying this much a month for a lease? I mean $7,800 a month? That's a whole lot", he says. Kara replies with affection, "Baby, I'd do anything for you!" PD hangs up the phone saying, "Okay, Babe. I'm going to have to run. I've got company."

PD and his fashion industry associate, Victor, are hanging out in PD's new apartment drinking wine and watching some pornographic videos together.

PD suddenly says, "Hey Victor. Mr. Victor Reese! My brother! I visited New York for Fashion Week last week." "Yes. You told me, many multiples of times." Victor replies not very impressed. PD says, "I hope that New York trip leads to something." "You know that I've started to really become fond of you, PD", Victor says changing the topic. PD boasts, "Well, you know that's not terribly unusual. I'm kind of likable and sexy. People are always drawn to me." He sniffles. "They're always looking at my ass." PD turns and suggestively twists his derriere back and forth in Victor's direction. Victor amused by PD, says, "Hmmm! This is kind of unusual for me. There's something about you that I find curiously perplexing." PD not understanding clearly, asks, "What do you mean?"

Victor ignores the question and asks, "Do you mind if I ask you a personal question?" PD replies, "I'm not sure that I can or want to answer any questions, but give it a shot." Victor let's his curiosity get the best of him and says, "I've been noticing that

28

you seem to take a particularly special interest in guys. In fact, it seems that you have a little too much of an interest in men for some people's taste. I never seem to see you express much of an interest in any women except in very rare cases. You don't seem to have much use for females. I was wondering... Are you gay?"

PD rejects all of Victor's speculation right off the bat, "Gay? What do you mean, gay? I could never be gay! Do you think I want to be like them? Victor simply asks, "Well, what are you then?" PD answers after a second of thought, "You might say I'm... fluid." Victor confused by PD's answer, asks, "Fluid? What do you mean? bisexual?" PD somewhat agreeing with Victor, "I guess you could say that, I have sex with women... and men whenever I get ready." Victor intrigued by PD, asks, "And which do you prefer?" PD teasingly replies, "Well that's something you'll have to find out." "What do you mean by that?" Victor inquires. PD smirks and says, "Well, I have been noticing the way that you have been looking at my ass."

PD turns and shows his buttocks again to Victor in a sexually suggestive manner. Victor chuckles and gives PD a line of cocaine as he snorts it. Victor replies agreeing with PD, "I have to admit that I've been kind of outdone with how handsome you are. I've never felt anything like this before, not in the whole fifteen years of my marriage or before then either!"

PD asks in surprise, "You mean you never have had feelings like this before? You've never cheated on your wife?" "I have a kind and magnificent wife! I love her, and I would never do anything to hurt her! I don't cheat. I can imagine that you find it difficult to believe that!", Victor replies. PD smirks and says, "Well then, why is your dick getting hard? I can see how hard you are, and obviously you're getting excited from looking at me. Let me see it!"

Victor asks, "See what? You mean like this? How much do you cost?"

PD says nonchalantly, "A couple grand." Victor reaches in his briefcase and counts out $2,000 cash and gives the money to PD. PD smugly says, "Thanks." Victor squeezes his engorged, erect penis, and shows the imprint of his penis through his pants in a way that is designed to induce PD's full arousal.

PD says with lust in his eyes, licking his lips, "I said, let me see it!" PD gets down on his knees on the floor and crawls across the floor to where Victor is. Victor pulls out his penis from his pants and shows how large it is to PD. Victor chuckles and says smugly, "Here! Take it! You know you want it!" PD plays with Victor's dick and says, "You see I'm rubbing it all over my face, my forehead, my cheek, both cheeks, my lips! See how I can kiss it like this? See how I can lick your balls?" He moans while he says, "My favorite!"

Victor totally turned on by PD plays along, "I can feel how erotic, how hot it is! You see when I rub it across your cheek back and forth like this how sexy it is? Come on! Close your eyes! Just take it, and suck it!" Victor slips his penis into PD's mouth. PD moans while taking it in, "Yes! Let me have it!" All of a sudden, PD opens his eyes as if he is startled out of a deep, hypnotic trance. He takes Victor's dick out of his mouth as if Victor's penis is literally burning hot and on fire, "Why did you do that? Why did you make me do that?" Victor surprised by PD sudden outburst, replies, "It just slipped. It just slipped into your mouth! I didn't mean to do it! You made me do it!" PD yells with anger, "You didn't have to make me do that you bastard! You're totally wrong for that, Victor!"

Victor still perplexed, asks, "Wrong? Then why did you get into it so much? Ask yourself that question, PD!" Trying to make a joke, Victor says, "You must be kind of a-dick-ted to that thing." PD disgusted by his jokes, "That's not funny, you're a sick fuck!" "I've never done anything like that before!" Victor replies. PD still disgusted says with a contorted face, "I can't believe you made me suck your raw, fucking dick with no protection whatsoever! I always use a condom for that! Victor patronized by PD's behavior, says, "Really? Well, I paid you for it didn't I?

Obviously, you're the expert at this, PD." PD replies in rage, "You can save the compliment, Victor! Your trifling two grand doesn't mean that much to me". Victor arrogantly says, "Riiiight!", exaggerating the pronunciation of the word.

PD runs into the bathroom in a fit of rage, gurgling loudly with antiseptic mouthwash. He returns and admonishes Victor, "Damn it Victor! I can't believe you made me do that! What are you, some kind of child molester?" Victor replies smirking, "What? What do you mean? You're a fucking thirty-six-year-old, grown-ass man! How in the world could you ever think that, like I'm a pedophile fucking around with a thirty-six-year-old grown ass man? Are you nuts?" Insulted, PD quickly realizes his mistake and storms off to his bedroom while Victor gets his clothes together to get ready to leave.

Victor tries to make his point again, "PD, if you didn't want to do that, you should have said so. You should've like told me to get the hell of here or something!"

PD still not taking any of Victor's preaching, "Well leave then! Get the fuck out! I'm going to tell your wife! Furious, Victor replies, "You're going to do what? Do it, and I swear! I swear to God! I'll kick your fucking ass!" Victor walks out of the apartment and as he slams the door, loudly.

CHAPTER 6—Daydreaming, the Rendezvous

PD and Kara are eating dinner together. As usual, he is ignoring her like a piece of furniture, and he is continuously on the phone. Kara is totally frustrated by his behavior, and she says, "I wish you would stop playing with that phone. Do you ever put it down?" PD, not taking much notice of Kara's comments, replies, "I'm not playing with it. I have to do my work, Kara. My work is very important. People depend on me."

As PD says that, he smirks and slips into a flashback, fantasizing about some of his many sexual escapades with men and women. Kara bringing him back to reality taunts him again, "Do you have to be joined at the hip to that thing, 24/7? You're like a teenage girl talking on that thing all of the time. We never have any time together; even when you aren't on that cell phone. Who in the hell are you talking to all of the time anyway—your bitch?" Exasperated, PD replies, "That's what I'm talking about. I'm conducting critical business and here you are complaining, always. Can I have any peace in my life?”

Kara still not taking any of PD’s insulting behavior, says, “So you're focused on what exactly?” PD rolls his eyes as he replies, “I'm talking about my work. You know what I do in fashion design. It's marketing. I have to connect!” he completes his sentence with a sniffle.

Kara replies not believing PD, “Well, actually, I'm not quite sure what you do. You could be anything for all I know. PD replies like a smart alec, “Right! How do you think I'm going to be able to be a fashion distributor without forming relationships with the right people? You're in this business yourself.” Kara still not stopping with her complaining says, “PD, you're on that phone even while you're driving. Driving and texting, among other things. That's why you're always backing into poles in the parking garage, and I'm always having to pay your car bodywork bills. Just keep it up!”

PD irritated by her now, replies, "Why do you insist on getting all up in my business? That's so irritating. If my driving gets me in trouble, then so be it, bitch." Kara says, "Have you ever thought that screwing around with the phone and driving might hurt other people too?" Kara tries to talk some sense into him.

Caught up in his own lies, PD's mouth twists at the corner as he denies the obvious "Hell no! I don't hurt people!" Kara rolls her eyes and says, "Yeah. Sure. Like you don't hurt me." PD quickly refutes everything, "Well of course I don't hurt you bitch. You're not a fucking person! You're my girlfriend!" Kara totally disgusted by the way PD Is talking to her says, "Right!" Kara looks at him as if he's crazy. She tries to continue eating dinner but, annoyed by him, she throws down her napkin disgusted and walks out.

As Kara is sitting in the restaurant, waiting for PD. She remembers multiple occasions in the past weeks where he blatantly stood her up. She leaves PD voice mail message after voice mail message, totally annoyed by his thoughtlessness. Given that he is late again today, she's oh so ready to read him the riot act whenever he finally appears. When PD finally does show his face, he acts as if nothing has happened; saying, "Hey Kara. What's up?"

Kara, thoroughly disgusted, replies, "What's up is the fact that you stood me up on three different occasions after you confirmed our date, you jerk. What is wrong with you? What happened?" PD, also annoyed by her complaints, says, "I got caught up in meetings, and that was it. I was meeting with clients." Kara replies with frustration, "Couldn't you call me at least?"

Utterly nonchalant, PD says, "What for?" Kara gasps at PD's insensitivity, "What for? PD, you have got to be the most inconsiderate, self-centered person that I have ever met in my life." PD, refusing to put up with any insults, replies, "And you are the most selfish girlfriend that I have ever seen in my life! I told you that I've been tied up with business meetings."

Kara chuckles in disbelief and asks, "Selfish? What kind of business is that?" As PD hears her words, he slips into a flashback state, recalling sex acts using his myriad toys. He does this with men *and* women. PD's eyes go blank as he further remembers one of his latest clients, Theo.

Theo, *"Let's go for a ride."* PD *flirtatiously asks, "Where do you want to go?" Theo smirks and replies, "How about somewhere we can kind of be alone? Don't worry. You don't have to sell your ass; not tonight, but I'll pay you for some anyway!" PD, intrigued by his offer, asks, "How much?" Theo thinks for a second and replies, "500". PD was hardly impressed by his offer and replies, "Not enough." Theo again makes an offer, "750."*

PD finally likes the offer and accepts it, "Sweet! I'm not sure that I'm up for that tonight, but I can use the $750." Theo asks, "By the way, what is your favorite sex act?"

PD's eyes twinkle as he replies, "Licking balls!" Theo laughs sarcastically and says, "Well you can lick mine any time." PD, intrigued by the offer, remarks, "You little slut!" Theo further teases PD, "Stick out that pretty little pointed tongue of yours! Stick it out, PD!"

PD quickly obliges his command, "Here you go!" PD sticks out his tongue, curls it, and makes sexually suggestive licking motions in the air and both of them laugh. The two of them then drive off in PD's navy-blue Cayenne, Porsche. PD quickly tells Theo to stop the car, "Pull over right here. Okay, let's get busy! Pull it out! Theo surprised by PD's sudden command says, "What do you mean?"

PD smirks and replies, "Don't give me that crap! You know what we came over here for! Let me feel it in my hand!" Theo instead demands, "Give me a kiss!" PD quickly wards off his demand, "What? Give you a kiss? What do you think I am? You know that I don't kiss men! I'm not going to kiss a man! You think I'm some kind of queer?"

Theo replies, "Well, yes. No, I just think you've got some pretty, sweet lips, and I want them, but I *want something else even more. Pull your thing out! Pull it out, man!" They both pull down their pants, and their erect penises jut out. They begin to mutually and intimately massage each other until each of them reaches a climax. PD says, "Let me shoot mine on my chest." PD and Theo groan loudly as they forcefully ejaculate! Theo satisfied by the experience says, "Damn! Here's some tissues! Help me clean up.*

PD awakens from his daydream and re-focuses his attention onto his lunch date with Kara. Kara clearly notices that he slipped into his own world and says, "PD, what's wrong with you? Are you there?" PD comes back to reality and replies, "Oh. Oh, I was just thinking about some business that I have to take care of." Kara lets it go and changes the topic, "Well, I want to talk with you about the trip that we took to Puerto Rico." PD, annoyed by her, asks, "What the hell is it, Kara?" Kara explains, "I really haven't gotten over the way that you insulted me. You called me a 'psycho'. Remember? I ran off mad and crying."

PD arrogantly speaks while constricting one corner of his mouth, "No, not really. I don't hurt people. I would never call you that! I never called you any 'psycho'! You must be losing it!"

Kara asks in disbelief, "Losing it? What are you talking about? On top of that, you stood me up at least three times when we were supposed to meet for several dates that you confirmed yourself. Your promises don't mean anything; not a thing! You called me a 'psycho', PD. That hurt, damn it!" PD annoyed by her complaining, frustrated replies, "Kara, you're always getting on my nerves. You always have some drama going on. I'm sick and tired of your sensitive bull shit! You know what? Faggot bitch! You make me sick!"

Kara gasps at PD's insults and stands up in the middle of the restaurant. She puts her index finger in PD's face in a threatening and angry manner, and pokes PD in the middle of his forehead. Kara glaring at PD, then says, "What did you call me? That's an insult! You've got some kind of nerve!" Kara then slaps PD and picks up a glass of wine and throws it in PD's face.

PD stands up, shocked that Kara ruined his designer outfit. He tries to wipe off the wine with a napkin from the table. Livid, PD says, "Damn, bitch!" Kara replies, "Here's your bitch!" She kicks him in the balls. Shocked by the unforeseen kick, PD barks, "She kicked me in the balls! Damn it! This fucking bitch is crazy." Kara's nose flares up as she says, "You haven't seen crazy yet, PD! Don't mess with me! Ever!" She then storms out of the restaurant in tears of anger and hurt.

CHAPTER 7—The Hunt and the Gala

The police department is busy as usual as Detective Cuffie and Davidson are completing paperwork and reading files when they come across information about Monica Saunders. Detective Cuffie says to Detective Davidson, "I've got an eye witness in Monica's death. I think it's the guy who a witness on the ground saw on the roof. The person of interest, I'm calling it, disappeared from the condo roof that night. I have a hunch that Monica's therapist can tell me something about this guy." Detective Cuffie calls Monica's therapist, Dr. Albert Sullivan, "May I speak with Dr. Sullivan." "Yes. This is he", the doctor replies in a professional tone. Detective Cuffie gets straight to the point and tells him, "I understand that one of your clients was Monica Saunders. I guess you know she fell from a building. I'm investigating her death, of course, and I need your help. I discovered a designer button in her hand at the scene of her fall when she died. I could use your help finding its owner. We think

44

the owner could be the killer because the situation looks very suspicious. I also need your help in connecting us with some of her old boyfriends? An eye witness saw one of what looked like her male friends on the top of the building when she died from the fall, and we want to talk to him." In cooperation with the detective, the doctor agrees, "Sure. Come down to my office at your and my convenience, and we can talk as soon as you are available. Just let me know and I'll work you into my client schedule."

PD is suffering through an emotional injury at this point after Kara crushed his ego in front of a boat load of people. Consequently, he failed to show up for work for several days which is what he normally does when someone threatens his very weak image of himself. Only his closest associates know about this pattern of his.

From a top down view, we see that PD is lying on his bed, naked, curled up on his side in a fetal position, sucking his thumb, obsessively overthinking the incident with Kara in the restaurant. As PD says, he's "in a funk." Killer, his dog, tries to pull off PD's bed sheets to get him out of bed to play. PD remains in his apartment, totally isolating himself from the world outside. He hears the phone ring and gets up to see the caller ID. He sees that his friend with benefits, Susan, is calling him and picks up the call and hears sexy Susan saying, "Hey sweetie! What's up? It's your *favorite* girl. It's Susan. Don't hate! Don't hate your cougar, your girl, Susan!" PD thinks for a second as his brain clicks back in from a heavy fog and he remembers saying, "My favorite?. . . Oh, hello, sweetheart. How are you?"

Sweet but flirtatious, Susan replies, "I'd be a lot better off if I could be with you again, honey. You know that I can't be without you for long, Babe, with your ultra fine, handsome-as-hell self!" In an instant as if injected with a powerful dose of adrenaline, PD's whole demeanor changes in response to Susan's flattery. He transforms into a totally energized, upbeat new character. He's fake as usual. He jumps up off the bed with the vigor of a circus performer executing a triple flip on a high wire and begins talking and walking around the apartment, still naked.

Susan continues, "I called your job, and they said that you haven't been in for two or three days." PD replies, "I've been out of it, kind of in a funk." Susan asks in confusion, "A funk?" PD replies, playing the victim, all beat down and pitiful, "Yeah. I've been kind of down lately, low energy, dealing with my crazy girlfriend." Susan replies, "You mean Kara? PD, now you know it's not like you to have woman problems." PD changes the topic and starts to build himself up in his typical self-aggrandizing fantasy world. He says, "Let me tell you about all of the cool business I've been involved with lately. Those Fashion Week people love me, the bastards." An hour passes while he's talking with Susan, mostly about how wonderful he is.

PD continues, "You know what? I got that bitch Kara to take care of our trip to Puerto Rico, all expenses paid. By the way, she's paying for my SUV and my fly apartment and stuff too! That girl's in love.

47

Can you blame her? I fucked the hell out of that bitch in Puerto Rico!", he says while smirking. He goes on, ". . . but I had to put her in her place, big time, at the restaurant for getting out of line. She tried to throw wine on me, but she tripped and spilled it on herself instead. I started to kick her in her balls". He laughs evilly, the compulsively lying MF.

Susan changes the topic in puzzled disbelief, "Hey PD! Guess what? I've got two tickets to the fashion gala at the convention center. You know good and well that gala would be a flop unless you showed up!" She strokes his ego, knowing from her many past intimate interactions with him that compliments are the key to get PD's engine in high gear. She goes on, "You've only got until next Saturday to come to the gala. I promise. I'll give you something good in return if you go! I'm going to kiss all over the head of that thing!" PD laughs smugly and replies, "What thing? . . . Oh, *that* thing. . . Okay. You convinced me!"

PD and Susan are snorting cocaine and
drinking as they stumble into the convention center.
PD boastfully says, "I know I'm going to kick some
tail, wrapping these fools around my little finger. Sean
Davidson is coming to the gala tonight? Damn! that
man is fine!" Susan asks in confusion, "Who?" PD
replies, "Sean Davidson, my boyfriend. Well, my
boyfriend, when he's in town, sometimes, maybe.
Whatever!" Susan asks, "How do you know that he's
coming here?" PD replies with his normal state of
overblown conceit, "Grapevine! PD knows it all!"

Susan chuckles and asks, "You're kidding! Isn't
Sean your favorite lover?" PD replies ambivalently,
"No, Kara is. No, it's Sean." Susan rolls her eyes and
says, "Make up your mind, bitch." PD, insulted by
what she called him, responds like a grade schooler,
which he is emotionally speaking. He tells her,
"Susan, don't you ever call me a bitch. That hurts, and
you shouldn't hurt people. You're supposed to be just
like me, you bitch!" Susan is surprised by his
contradictory words and replies, "Of course, Baby!

49

You make up a lot of rules that you don't follow, don't you? It's all about you. Now, let's check out the gala."

A long line has formed leading into the gala ballroom. PD grabs his cell phone as if deep in conversation as he breezes ahead confidently to the head of the line. Feeling entitled, PD says to Susan, "Susan, I know you don't think I'm going to wait in this line, do you? Check this out." The security agent stops PD as he tries to cut the line and get in and says, "Hey man, where are you going?" PD replies arrogantly, "Ask Sean Davidson where I'm going." Totally confused, the security agent asks, "Sean Davidson, the actor?" PD smirks and says, "Yes, my number one closest friend, Sean. Mind your own business." The security agent looks frustrated as PD motions to Susan to come on to the head of the line. He then takes Susan by the hand and drags her into the ballroom while she gawks at him. He escorts his lackey, Susan, to the table and caresses her around the nape of her neck. He kisses her softly on the cheek. PD says, "Girl, you sure are fine. Come on sweetheart."

Susan swoons and replies, "OK, baby. Just make sure that you include me in *everything* that's going on in here. You know I have to touch bases with at least a few of these so called top-shelf industry people. I might even be able to get some hot, young dick from some of these green horn bastards in here in the process." PD laughs and says, "Got you! You're a slut!"

As they are laughing PD's phone rings showing the caller ID screen, "Shush! Be quiet. It's Kara! I told her that I was going to take my cousin, Josh, clubbing tonight." PD answers the phone, "You, sorry bitch, didn't I tell you not to call me again tonight? I'm hanging out with my cousin. Don't call back here. Damn!"

Kara replies, crying, "PD . . . !" He cuts her off and hangs up the phone. PD shouts, "Can you believe that bitch is trying to track me down?" He starts his trademark fidgeting, pacing, and walking around the ballroom. PD exclaims, "Hey, baby. Susan. I just talked to the chairman of the chamber of commerce, Mr. Emerson. That man loves me! I think he was admiring my ass! Hold on. I'm going to wash my hands."

He leaves the ballroom and goes to the men's restroom. PD enters the VIP men's restroom and relieves himself at the urinal. He notices a familiar face beside him, "Well, if it isn't sexy Sean. What in the hell are you doing in here?" In an attempt to entice PD, Sean replies, "I'm in here waiting for some excitement. That would be somebody like you, PD! What are you doing here?" PD sniffles and answers, "I guess you'll find out."

PD locks the door to the restroom behind him so that no one else can come in and remarks, "It's been a long time since we've been like this, Sean." Sean agrees, "I know, Mr. PD. I've missed you. Did you miss me?" "I don't miss people. I missed this!" PD replies as he shoves his hand into Sean's pants and starts to stroke his private parts while using his other hand to reach around and grasp aggressively the cheek of Sean's buttocks. He further continues, "Come here! Did you bring the protection, the Magnum?"

PD walks diagonally while continuing to grasp one cheek of Sean's buttocks and, walking sideways, maneuvers both of them toward the handicapped stall. After 10-15 minutes of erotic maneuvers in the handicapped stall, they break free from their risky sexcapade, and PD and Sean emerge from the restroom. PD offers Sean, "Come on into the ballroom and sit with me and my friend, Susan. We might as well make it an evening." Sean accepts the offer, "Yeah, sounds great!" as they walk towards where Susan is sitting.

CHAPTER 8—Cougar Power

Susan invites PD and all her friends to her apartment for some twisted fun. Everyone's busy talking and laughing as Susan asks, "Anyone want a cocktail?" PD answers with childish excitement, "I do! I do!" as he sniffles from his emerging cocaine affection. Susan replies, "OK, baby. Come on over here, and get something to drink." Several people, including PD, are snorting cocaine. Susan gives PD a drink. Choking, she hands him a very strong joint too and asks, "How about taking some of this?" PD replies making a face, "I don't smoke pot. That's for big, fat, pussies like Sean!" Sean replies smiling sarcastically, "Ha, PD!" PD takes several puffs off the joint and then he takes a sip of his cocktail. PD then exclaims, "Wow! This drink's fucking amazing! Whoever made that knew what the hell they were doing!" Susan replies flattered by the compliment, "Yes, PD. It was me who made the amazing drinks.

Linda then suddenly says to everyone, "Hey everybody! Do you all mind if I watch you guys get it on in Susan's boudoir? Sean chuckles and replies, "This is part of my personal harem for all of my bitches, including PD." PD smirks and says, "That's oh, so, funny Sean. Now get over here." PD and Sean gaze squarely in each other's eyes, and with a drink in one hand, PD places his arm on Sean's shoulder. Sean then in an attempt to allure PD says, "Let me kiss those sweet, juicy lips of yours." PD sighs and replies, "You know that I don't kiss men, you, homo!" Sean says, "You're a walking contradiction, PD." PD actively snubs him and his statement as he replies, "So?"

Susan then changes the topic and invites everyone to participate in a private party for the group in the bedroom, "How about everyone join me in my boudoir! Now!" They all shuffle quickly into the bedroom where they prepare for an orgy. Susan smiles with vile and says, "It's time for some action. PD, you're all mine this time, Babe ". Everyone climbs into Susan's oversized bed as they all make love to each other passionately. After an hour or so, when they are free from their nondescript sexual rendezvous, Linda says, "Let's go get cleaned up and head to the living room so we can talk." Everyone agrees and replies, "Okay."

Police personnel are briskly walking around the office. Detective Cuffie says to Detective Davidson, "Hey, Rob. Come check this out." Detective Davidson comes closer and asks, "What's up?" Detective Cuffie says with a pleasant look on his face, "I think I have a lead on that case we talked about." Detective Davidson replies, "You mean the one involving your goddaughter, Monica? She fell off the roof while they were filming that party piece for fashion week, right? Detective Cuffie says with a frown, "Awful doesn't begin to describe it. I started looking through Monica's things and came across some photos of some guy. He's wearing a swanky jacket in the photo very similar to that button we found in Monica's hand when she died. I'm going to check Monica's social media accounts and see if I can find out who he is and talk to her therapist. She told me that she's seeing a Dr. Sullivan." Detective Davidson then offers his support, "Don't worry. You've been through enough with your goddaughter passing away. I'll check it out for you." Detective Cuffie expresses his gratitude, "Thanks, Rob. I really appreciate that!"

The next few days run quickly by as Detective Cuffie and Davidson cast a broad net conducting the investigation into Monica's death. They create a sociogram which lays out all the people closest to Monica. They then work together to scour the neighborhood for clues about Monica's death. Of course, PD was on the sociogram, and since he closely resembled the person identified on the roof, they narrow down his identity for further investigation. They interviewed PD's mom, Carletta, as part of the extended investigation since PD was involved with Monica before her death, and Carletta knew that. Also, Monica's journal suggested that she was in love with PD along with her written admission that she is pregnant. Detective Cuffie gained access to the journal as part of the investigation which confirmed his suspicions.

Carletta tells Detective Cuffie all she knows and more about PD because, being a narcissist herself, just like her son, she doesn't mind throwing PD, whom she loathes, under the bus. Why does she hate PD? She deplores PD because he reminds her of his deadbeat, alcoholic father who jilted and abandoned her while PD was a baby. For many of PD's early years of development, she would tell PD, "I hate you. I wish you were never born. I should have aborted you. You're just like your sorry ass father. You'll never be anything! You're worthless." Carletta treated PD like this day in and day out for years because as a narcissist, PD was a pawn on her little chess board of life. As far as she was concerned, he was like an object to be controlled, manipulated, and criticized, and she got a rush from that. He and anyone else around him who could be a good target was her go-to source of self-validation. By putting him and everyone else that she could down, she built herself up, or so she thought.

Carletta invested considerable energy into screaming and yelling at Young PD while constantly berating him with the most despicable forms of insults and profanity possible. Young PD's solution to the emotional abuse was to go inside his head, embrace addiction, entertain depression, escape emotional danger, or some combination thereof. PD decided to go inside his head and lie to himself about himself. The more lies he told, the more he believed his lies, and at some point, there was no coming back. He was trapped in his own web of internal lies which he transformed into a façade that he showed the world, avoiding exposure of his true self at all cost.

What's more, throughout his entire childhood, his mother never once told him, "I love you". The only thing that she liked about him was his exceptionally good looks because she could brag to her friends about how handsome he was, building herself up as the source of this asset. Putting PD's good looks on a pedestal to her friends behind his back, but never to his face, was a source of narcissistic reinforcement for her. In other words, it was a way of filling the black hole that she called a heart. Perhaps Carletta's abusive and neglectful child rearing practices contributed to PD's pathological self-centeredness.

Staying true to her callous MO toward PD, Carletta tells the detectives how PD must be behind all of this chaos, Monica's death, etc., and that she wished she had aborted PD at his conception. It's hard to imagine how a parent could do such a thing, but it's not unusual for a narcissist to place the children in jeopardy. Deep down in her heart, she knew she hated him because he reminds her of his father— mannerisms, voice, and looks—but in the public she acted as if she adored him.

Detective Cuffie and Rob read between the lines and find it really weird that a mother has so much hatred for her own child. There must be something wrong with her, but what? After interviewing Carletta they move on as they interrogate several others from the community and then go to Dr. Sullivan to further discuss the case.

Everyone is sitting around Susan's living room talking when PD's phone rings again. PD twists the corner of his mouth, makes a face, and picks up the call, "Hello, Babe. I was just thinking about you a few minutes ago. Can you meet me for coffee?" Kara replies, "I need to talk to you. What time do you want to meet?" PD says, "How about noon? Oh yes, I thought you might be interested in going to the Jazz concert at the museum. Let's talk about it at lunch tomorrow." Kara agrees, "Okay". PD then hangs up the phone.

Susan upon hearing the conversation, asks, "Who was that?" PD replies smirking, "That was my famous landlord, Kara!" Linda says in confusion, "I thought Kara was your girlfriend." PD chuckles like a minion from hell and replies, "She's my fucking landlord/bitch/girlfriend. By that, I mean she sucks my dick, and pays the rent on my $7,800 per month

61

apartment. That's a lot of fucking rent for an apartment." Susan stays quiet for a second and then cautiously says, "You shouldn't trust Kara. I hear she's been asking around town about whether you're gay." PD is agitated upon hearing this and says in a slightly loud voice, "I'm not a homo! You hear me?! I'm not a homo!"

Susan replies assuring PD, "Yes, PD, I get it! You're not a homo! Do you really trust her? You better strike first before she can do some serious damage to your reputation! I have a little something to give you as an insurance policy against her smear campaign." Susan pulls out a small, lighted storage box, and inside of the box is a dazzling amulet, shaped like a diamond. PD, impressed by the piece of shining jewelry, replies, "Nice!" Susan says, "It's nicer than you think. Not only is it an amulet, but it's a wireless gadget for spying on people like that bitch, Kara. It can pick up and record every detail of a conversation. I mean it can pick up *every* detail. Give it to Kara. Have her to keep it in this storage box, though. You can keep track of her every move. You can even keep an eye on her appointment calendar with the app. Just get her password." PD is totally intrigued by Susan's warped resourcefulness and replies, "Are you serious?" Susan smirks and says, "This piece cost me a pretty penny. I hate to say this, but I'm as serious as a heart attack."

CHAPTER 9—Jazzy Betrayal

      PD and Kara meet for a date in a restaurant after a month or so. Kara greets PD by hugging him and saying, "Babe, it's been a long time. I thought we'd never get together." PD constricts the corner of his lips. This is what PD does whenever he is getting ready to tell one of his monumental lies. He replies, "Yes, I know, but I've been so busy. People have been hanging all over me, trying to get me to work on their projects. Oh, yes. Remember we talked about going to the museum for the jazz concert? I hear that the band is great! Let's go?" Kara agrees and asks, "Okay, when is it?" PD says, "It's kind of short notice, but it's this coming Friday. I'll scoop you up at 8:00 pm, and I'm going to be on time this time; so you be on time. Just look for my Cayenne." Kara says sarcastically, "Your Cayenne? Oh, you mean the navy blue one that I'm paying the note for every month? I'll be on time as usual, PD. Remember you're the one who's always late or either a no show." PD shows his irritation and replies, "Stop the fantasies, Kara. Here! I have something for you." He takes the dazzling amulet out of the storage box and puts it around Kara's neck. Kara, surprised by PD's beautiful gift, gasps and says, "Oh my goodness. It's superb!" PD conceitedly replies, "Would you expect anything less from me? It's not half as superb as you are!", pure manipulation. PD flattered Kara successfully with the compliments and the gift as anticipated. She exclaims, "I'm never going to take this off!" Thinking that he is some kind of genius, PD says, "That's the thought! Keep it in this storage box, Babe." He made a point of it to remember what Susan had said about the amulet, "Tell her to keep it in the storage box." Poor Kara is elated.

Kara says after a moment of silence what she has been trying to tell PD for a long time, "PD, I know that this is not the best time to say this, but I'm going to see a therapist." (There actually is no good time for her to tell PD anything sensitive because he usually deflects or shuts down the conversation.) PD asks her, "What for?"

Kara replies, "It's our relationship. We're just not the same like when we were in Puerto Rico, except for your little off-color statements about me when we were there. Something is not right. Will you go to therapy with me?" PD, throwing all the shade he can at her, says, "I thought Puerto Rico wasn't that cool either. You threw driftwood at me. You were ridiculous! You do need to go to a therapist, you mental case, because you are kind of crazy." Kara insulted by his allegations replies, "Damn! Now you're a therapist! Where's your license? What do you mean? I'm crazy? That's another one of your insults."

PD sniffles and replies, "Well, not crazy. I said kinda crazy. Crazy is as crazy does. You put up with my ass. Don't you? . . . You *know* that's crazy!" Kara rolls her eyes in annoyance and replies, "There you go with one of your asshole statements again. You do something nice, like give me a fine gift, and then you ruin it with your big, fucking, inappropriate mouth. How about if I stop paying on that high class apartment of yours and that damn SUV? You know what, I'm going to stop paying your rent and the payment on that Cayenne unless you get an evaluation for counseling."

PD quickly replies, "I'll think about!" He looks at Kara and sees her glaring at him says, "Okay, okay! I'll go, but I'm not paying for it." Kara, irritated by his greediness, replies, "Believe me! I'll be happy to pay for it! No question!" PD gets mad about what he considers to be Kara's insulting behavior. The least slight, intended or not, insults him, and Kara ends up walking on egg shells. He gets up and yells at her, "I can't stand any more of your fucking nagging, you fucking simple ass whore." Kara goes off, "You know what? I've just about had it with you, you cocky, inconsiderate asshole."

Kara tries to slap him, but he stops her by catching her hand in the air. Kara, not taking any more of PD's bullshit, surprises him by slapping him as hard as she can with her other hand. PD says in furious disbelief says, "You a fucking bitch!" Kara chuckles in anger and replies, "If anyone is a bitch, it's you." Then she shouts at the top of her lungs, "You, homo punk. In fact, I've been thinking about spreading the word all across this city about your punk ass! You think I don't know? I know everyone in this town." PD is not scared of her threats. He replies, "Know what? Try it, and trust me! I'll pay your ass back." Kara huffs and runs out but returns shortly afterwards pointing a finger at PD, saying, "I'm going to send you the name and address of the therapist, Dr. Sullivan, and you better show up on next Thursday at 3:00pm, or you are going to be homeless and riding public transportation."

After a few days Kara places a video call to PD to apologize. She wants to repair their relationship if possible. PD picks up the call, and Kara says, "How do I look? Messed up? Sorry about the restaurant, but you made me so mad. Sorry!" PD notices that she looks beautiful on the videophone screen but ignores it and replies, "You ought to be sorry. You're always doing something, Kara. Slapping me in front of all of those people? Talk about embarrassing. Forget it. Forgiven." Kara smiles and says, "You're so concerned. It's all about the way you look. Anyway, love you so much, PD."

PD makes a face and replies, "Yes, I know! Why do you always have to be so mushy? It's creepy. Anyway, yIIou ready for the concert?" "Sure." Kara replies. PD says, "See you tomorrow night then." "I'll be on time." Kara replies and ends the video call.

Urban sophisticates are milling around the common area of the museum. Contemporary jazz is playing. PD and Kara are drinking cocktails with the rest of the museum patrons. PD is fidgeting, as he says, "When are they starting the jazz? It's awesome." Kara agrees and replies, "Yes, my friends say the same thing. This cocktail isn't bad either." PD sniffles, and asks, "Uh huh. Would you like another one? Kara nods her head and says, "Yes, Please. Peach daiquiri". PD replies, "Okay. Let me get it." as he turns around he asks her, "Kara, got any cash?" Kara replies, "Here. Fifty dollars. Hold onto the change."

PD saunters over to the bar to purchase the drinks. In the meantime, a young man strolls by and notices Kara. It's Adam Walls again. Adam walks towards Kara and says in a happy tone, "Kara, Kara. Hey! It's Adam. I told you that we'd run into each other. Girl, that dress is ravishing. It's nowhere near as great as you though." Adam kisses Kara on the cheek. From across the hall, PD sees Adam kiss Kara, and he goes wild with jealousy. The bartender gives him some bills in change, and PD balls up the bills in anger upon seeing them talking together.

Kara flattered by Adam's compliments, replies to him, "Oh, thanks. It's one of my favorites. You look pretty good yourself, Adam. Adam grins and says, "I thought we'd have lunch again." Kara apologetically replies, "Of course. I've been busy. Call me on Monday."

PD sneers at Kara and Adam as he balls up the change in dollar bills in anger. He returns to join them. Interrupting their conversation PD says in a jealous tone, "Well, who do we have here?" Kara replies, "Oh, PD. Remember Adam, from Puerto Rico. You know, the guy from work." PD says narrowing his eyes slightly, "Yes. Interesting!"

Kara continues, "Remember, we saw him playing Frisbee?" PD hands Kara the drink. Several dollar bills are crumpled in PD's hand. He crushes the bills and lets them fall on the floor. PD replies, "Oh, yes. Hey, Adam, how have you been doing?" Adam simply replies, "Same."

PD then tries to get away from Adam by saying, "Well, Adam. I think we're going to have to get moving. The concert is starting. Pleasure to see you again." PD grabs Kara's waist as he says, "Come on, Babe." and enter the concert area. As they get out of earshot of Adam. PD says, "I guess you're pretty happy to see your boyfriend again. He was all over you. I was checking it all out! You thought I didn't see you, didn't you?" Kara surprised by PD's false allegations, replies, "All over me? What do you mean?

71

We were just talking. There's nothing else to it." PD doesn't believe her and says, "Right! Nothing to it? You might as well have been grinding in the hallway. I don't like him. He's a dick, trying to take my girl. I'd appreciate it if you'd stop flirting with him." Kara looks at him as if he's crazy and replies, "If you want to know the truth, and I'm sure you don't, it looked like you were flirting with him more than anyone in Puerto Rico. Remember that?" PD gets embarrassed as they are in public, "Remember what? Kara, you must be losing it. What do you think I am, some kind of homo?" Kara sarcastically replies, "At first you thought he was sexy. Okay, PD. Have it your way. You didn't flirt with Adam in Puerto Rico, and him and I were grinding pelvis to pelvis and having sex in the museum hallway tonight in front of hundreds of people. Oh, yes, and you're not attracted to men like Adam."

PD, annoyed by her, says, "Cut the crap, Kara. You know what you did. Why don't you just own up to it. You pissed in my face tonight!" Kara rolls her eyes and says, "Sure, PD. Whatever you say. I do everything wrong. You're perfect. I get that! Okay PD, how about I apologize since I'm always walking on eggshells. I'm sorry."

PD smirks and replies, "That's more like it. Now, let's go inside before we miss the concert." Inside of the concert area, everyone is thoroughly enjoying the performance, clapping their hands, smiling, and appreciating the performance. Kara says gleefully, "Isn't this great?" PD replies agreeing with her, "Yeah, they're awesome. Remind me of days when I used to be part of a slamming band. Too bad I had to move. Wait, let me sing something for you."

PD sings a chorus of Marvin Gaye's hit song from the 1970s, "You're All I Need", to Kara. Staring her in her eyes, she melts inside as she's overtaken with flattery. Kara happily exclaims, "Oh, PD. You're so sweet! I didn't know that you could sing." PD smirks and says, "There's a whole lot about me you don't know."

PD's phone rings. He checks it and reads a message from Susan. *Hey Baby. I need you to meet me at our favorite spot, the resort. Right now, honey I need your help, come on."* Kara notices PD and asks him, "Who was that? I mean the text message." PD twists the corner of his mouth and replies, "One of my business partners wants my advice on a business deal and wants me to come now."

Kara asks in disbelief, "Come now? You mean you are going to leave me? Here? At this concert by myself?" PD nonchalantly says, "Oh not a problem, I'll call you an Uber. You're not going to be able to get in contact with me for a couple of days. I'll call you." They say bye to each other as they part ways and PD goes to the resort to meet Susan.

CHAPTER 10—Sex Play

PD and Susan are drinking, laughing, and chasing each other around the private suite at the resort, like giddy children. PD says flirtatiously, "Hey girl, bring your pretty cougar ass over here. I didn't come all the way out here to this place for nothing." Susan replies, "Why don't you come and get me, handsome, and who are you calling a cougar?" PD licks his lips and says, "I bet you call all of the conceited guys handsome. I'm going to have to tame the cougar."

Susan bats her eyelashes and asks, "And how are you going to do that, handsome?" She start rubbing PD's chest and play with his nipples. PD laughs and replies, "Stop! That tickles, you little fine ass whore." Susan seductively says, "I'll show you whore. Give me that big thing of yours, or I'm going to have to take it." PD replies, "Wait a minute. I have to call Kara."

Susan rolls her eyes and says, "Kara? Why do you have to spoil all of the fun? Kara's a sorry excuse for a human being. Now get your fine ass over here to your mama cougar." PD replies, "Now, Susan. You know that I have to keep the peace with Kara. She's paying for my apartment, my SUV, and over half of all my other expenses. Do you want me to give all of that up? That girl's in love! I need to call her ta check in. She threatened to cut off my cash unless I go to therapy." Susan says, "Okay but you know I can give you money like Kara does." PD shook his head and replies, "Well, Kara, unlike you, is still kind of innocent. It's that Je ne sais quoi, that special little something that draws me. I love a challenge. Anyway, she puts up with my shit, my moodiness. It's a little sick, but so what? I get a charge out of it."

Susan smirks and says, "Okay, but you better come back here when you finish talking to her." PD dials Kara's number on his phone and waits for her to pick it up. Kara hears the phone as she is walking in the door of her apartment. She rushes to the phone and picks it up. PD says, "What's going on, Kara? How are you doing? I just thought I would check in to see what you're up to." Kara replies, "I was just walking in the door. Hold on. I need to put a few of these bags down. Okay. I'm here. What are you doing? How's your business trip. I miss you." PD replies smugly, "It's going great! I think I'm making some pretty deep, up close, and personal contacts with people that I'm kind of into. Pretty soon, I'm going to get deep into it."

PD makes seductive gestures toward Susan. Kara asks, "Oh, really! Well, who are you hanging out with?" PD lies, "I was hanging out with Victor, but I'm not sure how productive that was." PD flirts while Susan is playing around with his butt and he tries to talk on the phone with Kara. He swats her away. PD continues, "Speaking of that, I hope you're not flirting anymore with that sorry tail, Adam. He's a hound! I have no respect for him. He's not only a womanizer, but he cheats on his women. Kara, you really need to stop spreading your legs for him."

Kara asks in disbelief, "What? What are you talking about? Are you really that crazy?" PD replies, "I mean men respond visually. I think you need to stop the charade and most of all the cheating. That's not cool, Kara! It hurts!" Kara, still in shock, asks, "It hurts you? PD, I'm not going to entertain any ridiculous comments like that. PD continues with his blame game, "You don't have to accept the truth, Kara. I'm trying to take care of some business here. Let me get off the phone. I have some people waiting."

He says this as he blows a kiss at Susan. Kara replies, "Okay, PD, but I'm not cheating or doing anything inappropriate. I don't appreciate your accusations!" PD quickly replies, "I'm not going to argue with you! I don't appreciate what you're doing behind my back. I'm going to get his ass. You wait and see!" Kara asks in confusion, "What do you mean?" PD replies, "Nothing. Anyway, let me run. I've got to get back to work."

PD abruptly hangs up the phone as Kara looks at the phone in disgust. PD seductively says to Susan while licking his lips, "Hey, Susan. You know it's time for us to get a little more into each other. Let me get rid of this phone." He pulls her closer and kisses her. Susan replies, "Sure, handsome." PD tosses the phone on the bed, and the phone auto-dials Kara by accident. Kara sees that the call is from PD and picks up the phone. Kara speaks but gets no answer. "Hey, PD. Is that you?"

While PD and Susan are having sex, Susan is making sexual sounds in the background and Kara hears it all. Kara says, "PD, what's going on over there? Who is that in there with you? It sounds like a female? Are you having sex? You better not be having sex with some woman there when you are supposed to be on a business trip." Kara quickly retrieves her digital recorder from her purse which she is using for work. She places her phone on speaker so that she can record what's taking place.

PD says to Susan, "Damn Susan, spread your legs. Spread them wide for daddy." Kara can't believe her ears as she hears PD and Susan having sex over the phone. "Oh, PD, PD! Give it to me harder, Fuck me." Susan moans. PD replies in a commanding manner, "Here Susan. Take it in deep! Okay, Susan. Shush! Be quiet, and let me get on top." He gets on top of her and starts grinding "Oh, shit Susan! That's some good pussy! Remember?" Susan asks in confusion, "Remember what?" PD loses track of what he's talking about and says, "Don't say a word so that I can concentrate. Lie still." Kara records the whole audio of sex act between PD and Susan.

Kara, after hearing PD's sexual escapade with Susan is extremely heartbroken and angry. She invites Adam to the park to discuss this matter with him as he's a good friend and she needs to get it off her chest. As Kara and Adam are having lunch in the park. She shares the incident between PD and Susan with Adam. Kara says, "Adam, I don't know how to tell you this. You know what? Over the phone, I heard PD having sex with his lap dog 'friend', Susan, yesterday." Adam, shocked upon hearing this, asks, "You're not serious. How do you know that they were having sex?" Kara replies, "They were panting and breathing all loud. The phone was on the bed. It auto-dialed me after he and I talked. He didn't know that I was listening."

Adam tries to console her by saying, "Maybe they were watching a wild video or something." Kara shook's her head and replies, "Adam, they were yelling each other's names out, very, very loud. He even told her to let him get on top and to be very still and quiet like he does to me when we are being intimate. He likes to be in control. Check this out." Kara takes out her digital recorder and plays the audio recording of PD and Susan having sex. Adam, after hearing the audio, raises his eyebrows and says, "Well, I guess that doesn't leave much to the imagination. They were definitely fucking! Fucking hard!"

Kara asks for Adam's advice, "What do you think I should do? Should I confront him on it?" Adam agrees and says, "I can't tell you what to do, but if it were me, I'd have to call him on it and let him know that you know about it. I'd let him know that you're no fool. Are you in love with him?" Kara looks down and replies, "I'm not sure that I know what love is anymore. This one-way 'love' is just too much for me to handle. I feel like an idiot, always walking on eggshells." Adam consoles her by saying, "Don't say that. You're far from being an idiot! You're brilliant, as a matter of fact! He's the dog!" Kara replies, "He says you're a womanizer and a cheater. Wait until I talk to him. I'm going to give him a piece of my mind!"

CHAPTER 11—Lighting the Gas

Kara decides to visit PD to talk to him about his relationship with Susan. She calls him and as he picks up, she says, "PD, what are you doing over there?" PD sniffles as he replies, "The usual. I'm just relaxing a little bit before I go out for the evening." Kara says in a serious tone, "I want to talk to you." PD asks, "About what?" Kara ignores his question and replies, "I'll be there shortly. (Twenty minutes later.) Buzz me in." Kara is standing at his front door. She pounds on the door. "PD. PD. Let me in! I said let me in. I want to talk to you."

PD gets up off the couch, throws his hands in the air in an annoyed motion, and says, "Just a minute. Hold your horses." PD opens the door and Kara comes straight into his apartment, livid. Kara crosses her arms and, in a very serious manner, says, "I need to talk with you about that 'business trip' that you were supposed to be taking when you abandoned me at the Jazz concert. You told me that you had an emergency meeting with a client, some guy. Susan is not a guy, PD. You're fooling around with Susan. Aren't you?" PD plays dumb and asks, "Fooling around?" Kara is totally incensed at this point as she replies, "You know. Having sex? So, you are going to say that I didn't hear you and Susan getting it on?" PD denies all the allegations by making excuses, "We were listening to some porno videos from her collection. You must be hearing things!"

Kara asks, "You call this a hallucination?" as she pulls out the audio recorder and plays the recording of PD and Susan having sex. PD asks, "What makes you think that's us?" She plays the recording. PD and Susan's sexual moans echo throughout PD's apartment on the recording, "Oh, PD, give it to me harder, PD! Fuck me. Here, Susan. Take me deep inside of you." Kara raises her eyebrows as she says, "You were saying?"

PD still denies Kara and starts the blame game, "I can't believe that you could manufacture a recording that you think sounds so much like me and

Susan. It must have taken hours in the lab to make our voices sound so life-like. As I think about it, actually, it sounds more to me like you and Adam fucking. I know that you have been fucking Adam, and now you try to get the heat off of yourself by blaming me. That's a good one! Kara, you're nothing but a fucking slut." Kara gasps upon hearing PD's false accusations, "How dare you call me such a thing. I've never betrayed you."

PD rolls his eyes, not believing her, and says, "Sure. Kara, we haven't been with each other for three weeks; so, in my book, we were broken up. Even if Susan and I hung out together, and we were not doing anything, it's not cheating. You and I weren't together at the time, Kara." Kara looks at PD as if he's crazy and says, "Yes, we were! So now you are saying that you did fuck her." PD replies, "I just said that you and I were not together. Anything is fair game. The fact is that you betrayed me with that rat, Adam. I don't want you to see him anymore."

Kara squints and says, "We haven't been seeing each other in the first place. We've had a couple of lunches, but the only other times that we have seen each other was in Puerto Rico and at the museum. Oh, yes. I did let him hear the recording of you and Susan having sex. He was disgusted." PD goes wild as he asks, "You mean you played that awful recording to a stranger? I ought to kick Adam's ass!"

Kara chuckles and replies, "I wouldn't try it. He's no wimp. Adam said that he had no doubt in his mind that it was you and Susan, fucking. At least he cares about me." PD sniffles as he replies, "Kara, you need to have your head examined, you and your boyfriend Adam. You have some nerve to point fingers at me when here you are whoring around all over town with Adam. Anyway, I'm going to have a relaxing dip in the hot tub." Kara asks in confusion, "What hot tub?" PD rolls his eyes as he replies, "Don't worry about it!" Kara throws her hands in the air in exasperation and says, "Do whatever you want, PD. You're confused to say the least. Yes, and you need to have *your* head examined. Adam's barely an acquaintance. You're a piece of work, PD." She huffs and runs out of the apartment, totally outdone with PD's attempt to turn the table on her.

Adam is very concerned about Kara and simultaneously furious at PD. He wanted to do what he could to protect Kara; so he decides to break into Susan's living quarters. He tries to find evidence to use against PD. Adam breaks into Susan's immaculate, high-end condominium compound. He jumps the fence and enters the main building where Susan lives. As he is doing this, he thinks, *I bet Susan has some dirty dealings going on in this hell hole. I bet Susan and that creep, PD, have some cocaine or something in here. I bet you! How dare Susan and PD treat Kara like that. I can't stand Susan. I've never heard of such a disgusting thing in my whole life. PD was supposed to be on a business trip. Some business trips. All he wanted to do was mess over Kara. I'm going to get his and Susan's asses.*

Adam sets off the private burglar alarm when he enters the compound which alerts PD who is in the hot tub relaxing after a strenuous workout. He is snorting a couple of lines of cocaine and enjoying the peace and quiet of the condominium while Susan is not there. PD detects Adam's intrusion on Susan's closed-circuit burglar alarm system. He sniffles and says to the dogs, "What is that? Is that the burglar alarm? Someone is in the compound. Let me check out the surveillance system. Fortunately, for her, Susan has the Rottweilers to protect the compound". It's not so fortunate for Adam, however.

All three of the Rottweilers are lying around the hot tub close to where PD is relaxing naked in the tub. PD speaks to the dogs, "Come here Rusty, Buster, and Clementine. It sounds like someone is in the compound. What do you think about that? Someone has broken into your house. Are you going to take that? Let's check it out." PD looks at each of the video monitors and discovers where the break-in has taken place. The intruder is in the west side of the building, and as PD looks at the video monitor he realizes Adam has broken into the complex. Annoyed, PD says, "Damn! That's Adam. What in the hell is he doing in here?" He then calls Susan, to let her know what's going on in her apartment. PD speaks, "Hey Susan, someone's broken into your compound. It's that Adam, Kara's boyfriend." Susan replies with a shocked, concerned response, "What? Are you Okay?" PD says, "Well, of course I'm Okay, but I'm not so sure that Adam is going to be Okay? Susan asks in a puzzled voice, "Adam?"

PD replies, "You know. Kara and I saw Adam on the beach in Puerto Rico. Kara has been cheating with that asshole. He had the nerve to stalk Kara, and he was all over her at the museum. He's been screwing Kara." Susan asks in bewilderment, "They're fucking?" PD asks, "Well, what else would Kara be doing? How about if I teach him a lesson.

I'm thinking about letting the dogs give Adam a warm greeting." Susan warns him, "PD, you know that could be dangerous, but on the other hand, the nerve of him. You might as well let my three children greet him, but I don't know a thing about it. You hear me?"

PD replies, "OK. . . How could you know anything about it when we didn't even have this conversation? Let me get moving", and PD hangs up the phone. PD opens the door to the main compound building, and the dogs run to the west side of the main building where Adam is. Adam sees the dogs coming straight at him and runs. "What the fuck? Oh shit!", he says in a perplexed manner as he tries to run as fast as he can to escape the dogs. He climbs up onto some tall furniture to get away from them. PD speaks to Adam on the public address system, "Hey, Adam. Is that you? I thought I recognized you on the video. Hey, man. It looks like you're dealing with some pretty ferocious canines there, I wouldn't mess with them if I were you. By the way, what in the hell are you doing in the building? Snooping?"

Adam replies in a haughty manner, "How is that any of your business?" PD responds, "Anything that happens in Susan's compound is my business. Susan's my friend." Adam replies, "Yeah, it sounds like you two are far more than just friends." Trying to act innocent, PD asks, "What do you mean?" Mocking PD, Adam replies, "I mean you're a rat!" PD says nonchalantly, "Thanks for the compliment, and for your outstanding performance, I have a special greeting from Susan's Rottweilers. Get him! Sick 'em!" The dogs start jumping up at the furniture to get at Adam. The furniture gives way, and he falls to the floor. The dogs surround him and begin to chew Adam up like hamburger. PD laughs, enjoying the gory event taking place, "Get him little doggies!" Adam is able to hold the dogs off for several minutes. The piece of furniture that Adam is standing on gives way, and he falls on the floor. The dogs overpower him. PD is watching the whole incident on the closed-circuit television system.

Adam groans in pain as he cries for help, "Oh, no, oh! Help! Help me! Somebody! Help!" The dogs grind Adam up with their teeth into unrecognizable little pieces. PD laughs mockingly and says, "Aw, can you believe it, Adam. You are dog's meat. Sorry for the tasteless humor."

PD then calls Susan again. He is a little shaken up over the gory scene he witnessed with the dogs and Adam. He says, "Susan, I hate to tell you this but there has been a terrible accident at your compound. Kara's lover, Adam, just got the shit chewed out of him by your Rottweilers." Susan laughs and says, "It serves Adam right! I never even met the boy, but too bad!" PD replies, "You didn't miss anything! Damn, Susan. You can't imagine what I just saw. I can't get it out of my head! It was way too much! I can't take this anymore." Susan says, "Do you think so? Go take a walk. You'll feel better."

He hangs up the phone fand goes for a walk. As he reaches the   park, distraught by the incident, PD is walking aimlessly around the park, pacing back and forth, and crying uncontrollably.

CHAPTER 12—The Mother of All Narcissists

PD's mother is walking around her apartment with a drink in her hand when she hears the telephone ring. She recognizes from the caller ID that it's PD. She picks up the call and PD says, "Hello mom." Carletta rolls her eyes as she says in a sarcastic tone, "Well, if it isn't my handsome boy." PD asks, "How are you doing, mom?"
She taunts PD, "How do you think I am? I guess you really care how I am. I haven't heard from you in months. Don't you think you could give me a call every once in a while? How are you doing?"

PD replies, "Not so good. I'm kind of upset. Well, mom. I was thinking about coming over to see you. You're right. I haven't seen you in a while." PD's mom scorns him, "I guess you want something. At least that's usually the case. If you want to come over, you better do it now, because I'm getting ready to go out with the girls."

PD replies, "I should be over there in about thirty minutes mom. I have something to tell you."

Carletta asks, "What's that?" PD replies nonchalantly, "Oh, it's not that important. I'll tell you when I get there." She replies snottily, "Okay, well hurry up. I don't have all night!" After twenty minutes, PD knocks at the door as his mom reluctantly opens the door. PD greets his mother, "Hello mom. It's good to see you again." She replies, "If it isn't my handsome boy. Let me look at you." She looks him up and down and frowns. "You're looking kind of thin and peaked in the face. You've been eating those pork chops again? You know it takes seven years to digest pork chops in your gut, your intestines." She scolds him showing fake concern.

PD rolls his eyes and replies, "Mom, you always say that. I looked it up. It takes 3-5 hours to digest a pork chop." PD's mom scolds him again, "Whatever boy, are you that damn stupid? Do you believe everything that you read on that godforsaken Internet? Anyhow, so what is it that you wanted to see

94

me about PD?" PD looks down and replies, "I've been doing a lot of thinking about some of the things that are going on in my life right now. I mean, it's my girlfriend. She's giving me hell." PD's narcissistic mom chuckles and asks, "You mean she's giving you what you deserve?" PD raises his eyebrows and asks, "What do you mean by that?"

PD's mom answers being brutally honest, "Well, if it's like your twisted escapades with your other 'girlfriends', usually what it means is that you have been screwing around on your girlfriend with some other little hussy and she's called you on it. I can imagine she's ready to kick your ass right about now." Offended, PD says, "Mom, you're always so hard on me." Carletta replies, "Right!!! PD, I'm no harder on you than what you bring on yourself. You're always screwing over somebody. So, what exactly happened?"

PD twists the corner of his mouth and replies, "Well, my friend Susan and I were having a business meeting at a resort. My girlfriend, Kara, claims that she heard Susan and me having sex on Kara's phone. I threw the phone on the bed, and it auto-dialed Kara by accident. That's when she says she heard us." Carletta looks at PD as if he's dumb and asks, "Business meeting? What kind of fool do you take me for? I can see the lie on your face. You were having a business meeting, and Kara concluded from a phone call that you were having sex with Susan. Were you and Susan screwing?"

PD replies, "I told Kara that we were checking out some porno videos that Susan got for one of her business ventures." Carletta rolls her eyes in disbelief as she asks, "You mean she was dumb enough to believe that bullshit?"

PD replies, "It gets worse. She actually has a digital recording of what sounds like me and Susan calling out each other's names while we were getting it on." PD's mom laughs mockingly and says, "Now, that sounds more like the real you. I can't believe it! Somebody actually caught you in your bullshit. That's a pretty smart girl!" PD asks in bewilderment, "Mom? I told her that there is no way that that recording could be me and Susan. How can you say that? Kara is talking about cutting off payments on my apartment and the Porsche. I really feel bad about what happened." Carletta replies, "Who else's voice would it be on the recording? You know you have a very distinctive voice. What do you feel sad about? Are you upset about the fact that you betrayed Kara or the fact that you got caught??

Panicky, PD replies, "She might stop paying for the apartment, mom! On top of that, she's been talking about spreading rumors about me all around town. Do you know what a disaster that could be?"

PD's mom says with ridicule, "Rumors? She probably thinks you go both ways. Smart girl! It sounds like she's got you by the balls this time, boy! You're just upset about getting caught." PD asks, "Whose side are you on anyway mom?" Carletta smirks and replies, "Well, in this case, I am on the side of what's right and what makes common sense, neither of which you have any. You might as well own up to it. You did her dirty. Be a man! Have some nerves! Tell her the truth and suffer the consequences! You're such a damn wimp, PD." PD worries, "I know, but she's trying to destroy me! I know she is. I can feel it in my gut!"

PD's mom laughs and makes a cutting joke about PD, "It sounds like you're going to feel it in your pocketbook pretty soon. That girl, Kara, means business! You might as well say goodbye to the fancy apartment and the Cayenne." PD says, "I can't believe you, mom! Don't you have any feelings for what I'm going through?" Carletta scoffs and replies, "Of all the people in the whole damn world, you have some nerve to ask about anybody having feelings about what you're going through, with your crazy ass. If it isn't the poor victim? The whole world is against you. Right?"

PD denies everything that he has ever done wrong and replies, "I can't help it if there's a bunch of jerks out there who criticize and can't appreciate me. I've sacrificed and helped a lot of people." Carletta frowns at PD's lying stupidity and replies, "What in your twisted mind would cause me to believe that you have so much to give the world or to care?" PD, not wanting to hear his mom's taunts anymore, says, "That's alright, mom. I'll just handle it on my own like I always do."

PD's mom continues to scold him in annoyance, "PD, you just need to stop being such a big, paranoid pussy and start taking responsibility for all the crap that you're always dishing out to everyone else. According to you, you can do no wrong. Grow up! That girl, Kara, deserves far better than you. You're a compulsive liar and a con man. You're just like your father, a no good, low down son of a bitch with no real heart for anyone! If that girl knows what's good for her, she'll high tail it for the hills."

PD asks, "Where is he? I'm going to find him. I have to. Since you're so sensitive to my situation, mom, I have another question that I have been meaning to ask you. Why did you send me to live with Uncle Mason in the first place?" Showing very little compassion, PD's mom replies, "Well, that's simple. When I had you, I was young. Your father was hardly ever there for us. The bastard. I just couldn't handle all of that responsibility living in the life. Being a call girl. Yes, Purvis, I had to sell myself to whoever, just to live. You didn't fit in the picture. I had to give you ta Uncle Mason for us to survive." Hurt by her comments, PD asks, "Did you know how bad Uncle Mason treated me? He used and abused me, Mom. He treated me like shit! So, how could you leave me with him?" PD's mom says, "PD, I was young! I was scared, and life as a call girl was no place for a child."

PD contorts his face as he says, "I guess that's not much different from me being a call guy, selling my ass to make it, after all that I went through. I was the victim!!!" PD's mom, without giving much regard to his hurt, replies, "Bullshit, Purvis! I didn't have a place to stay, and I didn't have a place for you to stay either. I thought that you'd be better off with a real man in your life, like Uncle Mason. Your father was anything but a man. I didn't know Uncle Mason that much. I didn't have any choice. I guess your situation was difficult."

PD scoffs and says, "Difficult? That's some way to put it! Mom, I realize you did what you thought was right, but you have no idea what I had to go through. Uncle Mason beat my ass. He destroyed me with what he said to tear me down. He hurt me and yes, sexually. I'll spare you the details."

PD's mom ignores what he just said as she says, "Let you tell it, everybody is always against you, and you have nothing to do with the results of your stupid choices! Just one stupid decision after another. You have the nerve to think that your girlfriend is at fault. You chose to sleep with that whore of yours. Wake up, Purvis! Be a man, and let Kara live her life!"

Two-faced, PD doesn't hear any of his mom's advice as he says, "You're no help! Mom you're such a hard ass. You know what? Fuck it then! I think I'll just take care of this bitch, Kara, myself! When I finish scratching up dirt on this bitch, she'll be on her knees begging for forgiveness!" PD's mom replies with disgust, "Wishful thinking, Purvis! When I called you an asshole, I meant it, boy! You've proven that you hold the title, asshole of all assholes. Congratulations!"

Sarcastic, PD says, "Thanks for the compliment, mom! Give me dad's address." She scribbles down PD's dad's address on a scrap of paper and gives it to him. PD says, "Thanks. I'll see you later!" Carletta replies with contempt, "Think nothing of it. Your father doesn't love you. He doesn't know what love is!" PD rushes out of the apartment in a fit of rage.

Parked on the side of the road, PD listens on the electronic listening device, the amulet that Susan gave him, as Kara is talking to her therapist, Dr. Albert Sullivan. Sitting beside PD on the passenger seat is a large leather brown valise. When PD hears what Kara is talking about with her therapist, he is irate as he says, "That bitch is starting her smear campaign against me with this fucking quack. I'm going to fucking get that bitch." Inside of the valise sitting on the passenger seat are four weapons. A razor-sharp hunting knife, a telescoping police baton, a three-pronged martial arts claw that looks like a carpenter's knife with long, sharp, curved teeth, a cellophane-wrapped package that says "C-4", an automatic handgun, and a storehouse of ammunition.

PD listens to the therapy conversation from his car. Kara asks, "Dr. Sullivan. May I call you Albert?" Dr. Sullivan answers in a professional yet friendly tone, "Sure."

Kara then starts telling the doctor everything about PD, "I've never seen anything like this before, Doctor. PD, my boyfriend, or whatever you might call him, is the most self-centered person I've ever met in my life. The whole world revolves around him, and let him tell it, everyone else in the world is the cause of all of his problems. Everything's black and white; no grey. He's gay, or something other than a regular guy, himself, I think."

Dr. Sullivan asks, "What makes you say that?" Kara stops and thinks for a second and then replies,

"He's always eye-balling men whenever we go out on a date. He lusted after my gorgeous friend, Adam in Puerto Rico. He's more interested in looking at guys than looking at me. In fact, I think he really hates women." Dr. Sullivan finds this interesting information as he says, "Hmmm!"

Kara then continues telling her story, "I think he hates me on some level! I'm the doormat. At first, PD treated me like a queen. Now he calls me "faggot bitch", "psycho", and who knows what when he gets mad. He's always mad, always irritated, and always trying to control me . . . He's not effeminate or anything at all; quite the reverse. When we're in bed being intimate, he's like a Greek sex god, but it's always on *his* terms. He's a man's man. He's hyper-masculine. I don't get this contradiction. I went through his phone, and what did I see? Believe it or not, I saw him and his friend, I think his name is Theo, lying in bed naked smiling, and hugging each other. It's too much! Maybe he's bisexual or something. He's always downgrading me. I got angry with him in the restaurant. I called him a homo. He went ballistic when I said that. And guess what? I kicked him in the balls." Dr. Sullivan amused by her, claims, "Oh, no! You didn't. Let me ask you something. Does he go off if you criticize him or get quiet when you disagree with him?"

Kara agrees and replies, "Off isn't the word— how about adult temper tantrums. He also gets really, really quiet when you disagree! What's really crazy is that in Puerto Rico, as soon as I told him I loved him, he started belittling me. It went from subtle rudeness to all out macro-insults in our relationship. I told him that his mother was right. He's an asshole. Everything definitely went downhill from there." Dr. Sullivan speculates as he says, "He exaggerates who he is to people? He lies all the time and hardly ever keeps the promises he's always making. Huh?"

Surprised, Kara says, "Yep! Wow! He's always talking about the fashion industry, the fashion industry and executives that he's friends with, like I care." Dr. Sullivan then says, "PD has no feelings for people, no matter who it is. He doesn't love anyone, not even himself, especially not himself. He's emotionally deaf. He's outdone when people criticize him about anything he says or does." Kara quickly agrees with the doctor as she says, "Yeah. You're absolutely right!" Dr. Sullivan continues to ponder, "He's hypersensitive. I think he doesn't have any balls whatsoever! A coward." Kara chuckles and replies, "Yep, he's kinda spineless. He can dish it out, but he can't take it. He's got skin like really thin tissue paper."

Dr. Sullivan says, "I have some ideas about what we may be dealing with. Let's pick it up next week at the same time?" Kara nods her head as she replies, "Okay, Dr. Sullivan." She picks up her bag and leaves the office after saying goodbye to the doctor.

CHAPTER 13—Demon Face

Detective Cuffie is reviewing some files in his office as detective Davidson rushes in and says, "Cuffie! I think I found something. It's that guy whose picture you were trying to match. His name is Purvis Dempsey. I think you might want to give him a visit." Detective Cuffie smiles in triumph as he replies, "Yes! I'll do that pronto. What's his number? I'll give him a call. Better yet, I'm going to drop by where he lives. Give me his address." After some time that day, Detective Cuffie knocks on PD's door, and PD opens the door and answers, "May I help you?"

Cuffie replies in a stern professional manner, "My name is Detective Anthony Cuffie, City Police. Are you Purvis Dempsey?" PD cautiously replies, "Yes, I am." Detective Cuffie says, "I need to speak with you for a minute. May I come in?" PD says, "Sure." Cuffie steps inside of the apartment and asks, "Do you know a Monica Saunders?" PD sniffles as he replies, "Kind of. We went out a few times." Cuffie looks intently into

PD's eyes looking for signs of deception in his face and asks, "When's the last time that you saw her?" PD replies without missing a beat, "It's been a while. Why?"

Detective Cuffie decides to stop beating around the bush as he replies, "She's dead. She fell off the top floor of the East Tower apartment building, not far from here. Do you know anything about that?" PD answers, "Hell no, detective." Questioning the truth of PD's response, Cuffie says, "How did you and Monica get along?" PD says back "Okay. We were just friends." Cuffie interrogates further, "Oh, just friends, huh? Your mom said that you and Monica Saunders were dating regularly at one point. Is this button yours? It's from your jacket, isn't it? Your mom and your fashion-forward tailor say that this custom button belongs to you."

PD replies disdainfully, "Yep. So, what. Mom doesn't know shit!" Cuffie responds, "Apparently, she knows something. That button was on Monica's body when we found her. You don't mind providing a DNA sample, huh?" PD asks snottily, "Why?" Cuffie asks, "Because Monica was pregnant. Did you have something to do with her death? If you were the father, the DNA sample would show it." PD defies Detective Cuffie, "No, and just being a baby's father does not make me a murderer." Detective Cuffie is taken aback at the word that PD used; so he asks, "Murderer? Where'd that come from? I'd like to ask you some more questions later."

Kara is in her apartment lying on her chaise lounge chair, relaxing as music plays in the background. The doorbell rings seemingly without end. Somewhat irritated Kara says, "Who is it? Who is it? Damn it, who is it?" When she answers the door, guess who it is. PD arrogantly answers, "Who do you think it is but your man." She opens the door and exuberantly exclaims, "PD!". They embrace, and he swings her around in a circle while softly kissing her over and over again. Kara says in a soft voice, "Baby, I missed you so much." PD replies nonchalantly, "Yes, I know."

PD lifts her up and lays her gently on the chaise lounge chair where he disrobes her completely. He kisses her all over her body while massaging her breast with one hand and rubbing her down with his other hand. He grabs her, bends her over, and has sex with her doggie-style. Kara moans. She can hardly stay still, "Oh PD, give it to me! . . . Oh, my God!" PD, as always, stops her, "Shush! Turnover. Quiet!" PD rolls Kara over on her back and enters her missionary style. Kara makes a melodious sigh and groans in pleasure, and PD stops her. Compulsively and mechanically focusing on his sex object, Kara, he exerts total control at all costs, "Be quiet! I need to concentrate."

PD has sex with Kara for several minutes until she explodes with multiple orgasms. Suddenly, he springs to his feet and masturbates fiercely on one side of the room. PD loudly groans with pleasure in a deep, sinister, growling voice as he reaches climax and ejaculates. He makes a demonic, contorted face when he explodes in ecstasy, and that scares the *shit* out of Kara. Terrified about what she just saw, she is paralyzed with fear in response.

Next, in a state of rage, PD says, "Damn, Kara! Look what you made me do. . . Damn it! Clean it up? Kara asks in bewilderment, " . . . What?"
PD replies with contempt, "I said clean it up . . . bitch? Oh, fuck! You know what? Forget it! Let me get the fuck out of here, you crazy bitch, and don't be pestering the hell out of me, you insane mother fucker!" PD rushes out the door.

Looking totally bewildered, confused, and perplexed, Kara closes the door and goes into the bathroom to take a shower. She returns later with a robe and towel on her head. Kara goes to her office and searches an online video on the Internet. She enters the first set of words that come to mind: "Narcissist", "psychopath", "egomaniac". Her facial expression conveys astonishment as she reviews the dumbfounding results from her search.

Several sessions later, Kara and Dr. Sullivan are sitting face to face as they resume their previous conversation from the last session. Kara is welling up with tears, confused and bewildered as she says, "Dr. Sullivan, I'm so exhausted, confused, and emotionally drained I don't know what to do! I'm walking on pins and needles, always. He came over the other night. We had glorious sex. Instead of ejaculating in me, he pulled out. He masturbated to climax on the floor in front of me. Then he blamed *me* for it, got mad, and stormed out. The face that he made when he reached climax looked like a demon straight out of hell. I almost shit myself! . . . Talk about worried. More like terrified!"

Dr. Sullivan raises his eyes in amusement and says, "Demon face? . . . . Hmmm. I've been thinking about your boyfriend, PD, and you, Kara, I'm not sure what's going on yet. This is speculation, but I think PD could be a narcissist. He also has features of other disorders in that cluster, cold and unfeeling. I fondly refer to people like him as "narcopaths." I kind of made it up."

Kara asks in confusion, "Narcopath? A cocky bastard?" Dr. Sullivan further explains as he says, "Well, a narcissist might be cocky, but most often they're wounded, emotionally impaired, and child-like inside. Number-wise, about one in every 25 people is a real narcissist, not like what you hear on T.V. It depends on who you talk to, how many there are." Kara exclaims, totally bemused, "Sounds just like PD to a T." Dr. Sullivan nods his head as he says, "Some therapists don't know what in the hell the word "narcissist" really means. He's toxic and most importantly, dangerous."

Kara grimaces as she asks, "You mean I've been dealing with a treacherous, maybe unsafe person this whole time?" Dr. Sullivan replies, "Whatever, Kara. Narcissism is a stone's throw from being a psychopath anyway. Sometimes, narcissism overlaps with antisocial personality disorder like Ted Bundy did-- the Florida sorority girl killer." Kara chuckles as she says, "I can assure you that I run across quite a few narcissists in my work."

Dr. Sullivan replies, "Yes, but this is different, far more insidious. He's more like a tornado in Kansas. Everywhere he touches down, he stirs up chaos." After a while, Kara says, "Yeah. I think he's afraid of being exposed, next to being abandoned or called 'crazy'." Dr. Sullivan replies, "Hmmmmmmmmmmm." Kara further explains, "He thinks I'm going to rat him out. Once, he called me a 'faggot bitch'." Dr. Sullivan looks amused and asks, "He called you what? 'Faggot bitch'? That's weird." Kara agrees but says, "I can't explain where that came from?" The doctor speculates, "He may be projecting what he thinks about himself onto you . . ." Kara asks in shock, "Seriously?" Dr. Sullivan warns her, "Uh huh. Dead serious. Be careful. The paranoid part of this thought disorder could be Ted-Bundy dangerous."

Kara says, "I can't believe he thinks I'm trying to destroy his fashion career. I can assure you. He doesn't really have a career in fashion as far as I know." Dr. Sullivan replies, "That's not surprising because he lives in a fantasy world." Kara says, "As long as I support him, financially, I'm worth something to him." Dr. Sullivan agrees. He says, "Absolutely! He's getting his rocks off by exploiting you. . . thinks you're a chump. I bet he's laughing at you behind your back." Kara replies, "Now, I get it, but I don't really want to get it. You say he's paranoid too . . . right?" Dr. Sullivan replies, "Deceitful, two-faced, paranoid, dangerous . . . Okay? Didn't you say that he thinks you're trying to destroy his career?" Kara nods her head and replies, "Yes."

Dr. Sullivan warns Kara again, "Don't be surprised if he tries to get you first. Just watch yourself. He may fall apart completely. I mean emotionally decompensate. The demonic facial expression you mentioned worries me. I mean it *really* worries me."

PD finally gets up the courage to visit his father at the address where his mother suggested. He has been dreading this moment, but he is still looking forward to meeting his dad out of curiosity. His father is staying at a cheap motel. He enters the motel and approaches the door of the room where his father lives. He knocks and sees that the door is unlocked. He slowly steps in. He sees that his dad is drunk as hell and half-way strung out on crack, it appears. He decides to wake him from his stupor. PD says, "Dad. It's me, PD." PD's father replies in a slurred voice, "Son? I don't have a son—." Frustrated, PD asks, "What do you mean. Mom told me . . . " Stone-faced, PD's father replies, "Mom told you a lie." PD pauses for a second and sheepishly tells his dad, "I need your help, dad. Just a few words to tell me . . . I need you to tell me . . . Do you love me?"

PD's father looks at him as if PD is from another planet, and in a slurred, angry voice his dad says, "Are you crazy? Get the hell out of here, you bastard. . . You're not my son, and I don't want to be bothered, boy." He then laughs and says, "Now give me my drink and, get the hell out of here, you son of a bitch." PD suffers another narcissistic injury from his father's callous, insensitive remark and walks out of the room, holding back tears at first until he can't hold it any longer. He falls apart, liberally crying from the hurt.

CHAPTER 14—The Dance & Revelations

Some months later, sitting in the Cayenne, Porsche, PD is listening to the private therapy session between Kara and Dr. Sullivan through the electronically bugged amulet. PD is outraged when he hears them talking about him. He pounds with tremendous force on the dashboard of the Cayenne, Porsche. He takes the three-pronged martial arts claw and rips up the calf-skin leather dashboard and says, "I'm going to fuck that bitch up and that fucking therapist too." Then in a childlike voice he says, "They're not my friends."

PD and Susan are driving just outside the city going northwest. PD is driving Susan's Lamborghini, and she is in the passenger seat. PD says in a coquettish manner, "Sweetheart, I'm glad we got some time to hang out with each other. By the way, what kind of car is this?" Susan simply replies, "It's a Lamborghini, Urus." PD asks with interest, "How much does it cost?" Susan thinks for a second then replies, "About $175,000.00." PD raises his eyebrows in surprise, "Wow, you got it like that?" Susan replies nonchalantly, "It's nothing."

Susan starts to rest her hand on PD's thigh and works her hand up to his crotch where she begins to rub his penis back and forth through his pants. She takes some cocaine out of her purse and they both snort a couple of lines of cocaine. She then continues to stimulate him, and he starts to get an erection. He begins to wiggle in his seat which causes him to lose focus on the road. The car is weaving back and forth slightly into the next lane enough to draw the attention of a state police officer who pulls up behind PD with his lights flashing, and the dash cam turns on automatically. Susan hides the drugs. The officer radios in the car's license plates, and pulls the car to the side of the road.

State police officer, "Sir, I noticed that you were weaving in and out of your lane since exit 32. I've been following you, and that's why I pulled you over. May I see your driver's license and registration." PD took out his documents, "Here you go officer. I'm sorry, my girlfriend was messing around with me. I guess I got a little distracted." After seeing his documents, the officer asks, "Please open your door, get out, and step to the rear of the car." The officer's headlights and police car spotlights focus on PD. He feels as if he's on a stage under a spotlight. The officer commands PD, "Please walk a straight line." PD asks, "Is this some kind of sobriety test?" The officer replies, "Yes." PD smirks and asks, "How about this?"

PD breaks into his Brooklyn, New York deep house club music dance. He skates to the left, right, left, and right. Then he twists his behind forward in a line, spins 360 degrees in a circle two times and breaks back into a house music line dance. PD is doing the house music dance when you look through the dash cam. The officer seems impressed by PD's dance. PD briefly gets down on the ground and spins and then flips back up vertically up onto his feet. He makes a two-step move to the left, right, left, and right spins one more time. He throws both hands up in the air as an extra cool signature gesture ending the dance. He smiles and pimps back to the car door. The officer follows him to the car door.

The officer is obviously entertained by PD's dance, so he lets him go. He passes the sobriety test. The officer says, "Wow! Awesome! Here's your driver's license and registration. Have a good evening, Sir." PD replies, "Thanks officer." PD and Susan get back on the road and continue driving.
PD says, "Hey, what do you say if you keep that promise that you made me? I mean the blow job. You promised!"

Susan rolls her eyes and says, "PD, you're such a sex fiend, you little bastard! . . . . Well, OK Babe." True to his typical high risk-taking self, PD drives the high-end luxury car while listening to voice mail memos and checking text messages. Susan goes ahead and gives him the blow job. Then Susan stops sucking him off when she sees that PD is trying to use his cellphone nonstop while driving. She tells PD, "You're going to have to get off that phone. If you aren't talking on that phone like a little teenage girl, you're texting; even while you're driving. You might as well get that phone surgically attached to your oversized head!" PD shuts Susan up by saying, "That's none of your business, Susan. Just take care of me like I asked, and let me drive!" PD moans and moans and moans as Susan blows him. He says, "Yes! Susan, do it harder." Then the phone rings, and he answers it, "Hello! Yes, it's PD. Hold up for a second. Ummmhhh!!! . . . Damn, Susan . . .You know that's sweet, girl! . . . Git it, girl! . . . I can't. . . can't . . . take it! Oh my God!" Susan continues to perform fellatio on PD, and he accelerates the vehicle. The car goes airborne. PD screams, "Oh shit! . . . Fuck!" Terrified, PD tries to gain control of the car. The Lamborghini flips three times before coming to rest on a bridge pylon. He crashes the care, just as Kara had predicted. PD and Susan miraculously escape from the Lamborghini with a few bruises and some minor scratches. PD totals the Lamborghini.

Furious, Susan asks him, "PD, what happened? You crashed my car, you asshole!" Ticked off, PD's response to her is just as annoyed, "What do you mean? You almost got us killed, and don't you ever call me asshole, hun!"

Susan gasps in exasperation, "You mean you're going to try to blame me for this? PD, don't you ever take responsibility for anything? If you hadn't insisted on texting and talking on the phone while getting a blow job, we wouldn't be in this mess. I'll call my insurance company. Let's get out of here!" PD simply replies, "Okay" like a spoiled little kid.

PD dials Kara's number while he's outside of Dr. Sullivan's office, "Hey Kara. It's PD." Kara replies, "Hello, PD. How's it going?" PD tells her, "I guess everything's okay. Well, not really. I have to tell you something." Kara asks, "What's that?" PD twists the corner of his mouth which usually means that he's getting ready to tell one of his colossal lies as he replies, "Two things. I was in a fender bender with my friend, Susan. That girl needs to stop texting and talking on the phone while she's driving. She's an absolutely terrible driver. She almost got me killed."

Pissed off, Kara replies, "You know I can't stand your little whore, Susan. You're still hanging out with her? After all of what you did with her on that *business* trip? I really can't believe you, PD. I guess you're still screwing her! . . . Huh?" PD acts dumb and asks, "Who, me?"

Kara goes soft, changes the topic, and asks, "I thought you said you were in a fender bender. Are you okay?" PD replies simply, "I'm fine, just a scratch or two." Kara says, "Great! Thank God! Susan's okay too?" PD replies, "Oh, yes. She's fine too. She's just a little shaken up." Kara says, "Well, whoop-de-doo! She should have broken her neck."

PD twists the corner of his mouth, and imparts his fantasy about the situation, "There's something else, though. It's the SUV, the Cayenne. I was parked at the library attending a workshop". Kara says, "What workshop?" PD: "Texting and driving. Anyway, some teenage kids broke into the SUV and totally trashed it. They destroyed that beautiful calf skin dashboard." Kara asks, "Are you serious? Why would they do that?" PD casually replies, "Oh, you know people these days. They're *all* crazy. I'm having the insurance company look into it, but I thought you should know." Kara tells him, "Okay, PD, but I'm in a hurry. I'm on the way to a meeting with my therapist."

PD asks, "Oh really. Who are you seeing?" Kara simply replies, "Dr. Sullivan." Then PD inquires, "You're still going to see that quack, Dr. Albert Sullivan?" Kara replies, "He's very well respected in the therapy community." PD says, "Well, I hope that I can trust you not to be talking about me any more behind my back and tearing down my reputation in therapy." Kara ignores him and says, "PD, I don't have time for this. I have to get to my meeting."

PD asks, "Where is your session? Maybe I'll meet you there." Kara replies, "PD, it hasn't changed. You know exactly where it is." PD says, "Okay, goodbye."

PD hangs up the phone in a mini adolescent temper tantrum, "You, sorry cunt! I know where your therapy session is. I know that you've been trying to fuck over me with that pussy, Dr. Sullivan. I've known about Dr. Sullivan and you for a while. I guess, . . . no I know that you're fucking *him* too. I hate that we have to see that quack together."

PD meets Kara at Dr. Sullivan's office and together they both go to the therapy session. Dr. Sullivan greets them as they enter, and he tells them to sit down and make themselves comfortable. Then he asks PD, "What brings you here today, Purvis?" PD replies, "You can call me PD. My girlfriend, here, Kara made me come. She threatened to take away my SUV, condo apartment, and everything else. Can you believe that? She's the most selfish person that I've ever met. She thinks I'm some kinda psycho. I don't hurt people."

Kara, surprised by his sudden negative outburst against her says, "No, not exactly. I think you need help. I believe what you just said is part of the problem. You're always coming up with some sick fantasy. Where do you get this shit? You blame me for what really comes straight out of your pitiful, mouth. You don't understand me because you don't give a fuck. I really can't take it anymore."

Smartass PD asks, "Can you believe that Doc? She thinks I'm a nut case." Dr. Sullivan notices the exchange between them and says, "Well, I have to be honest with you and cut to the chase. If what she is saying is true, it looks like you can use some emotional support. Let me ask you something. I know it's sensitive, but I have to ask. Were you physically, sexually, or emotionally mistreated as a child?"

PD thinks, *This is where I manipulate the hell out of Mr. Genius—therapist. I know far more than he'll ever know about this therapy shit. I'll give him my oh-woe-is-me act.* PD says, "Actually, I went through all three of those experiences, and believe me. It was no walk in the park, as they say. My Uncle Mason and my brother, Martin, abused me over a period of years. Plus, as a child, they pimped me out to the monstrous sex perverts where I lived. I'm still struggling with that shit." PD thinks, *No joke. They actually did do that—beatin' my ass and, if that wasn't bad enough, makin' me their neighborhood whore! The Bastards!* Dr. Sullivan continues, "PD, these experiences may have changed the way you look at the world. Depending on who you talk to, one in 25 people are like you. I think you're terrified of the psychological demon inside of you! Your inner demon is like a pretty, little Easter egg with a charming red bow on top. The problem is that when you open up that alluring, make-believe package, you see nothing but a moldy, brown object filled to the brim with a maggot-infested, rancid black sludge that represents your soul, psychologically speaking. That twisted essence is the 25th demon that you think you really are deep down inside. That's how you really see yourself! It's your dirty little secret." PD answers, "That sounds like psychobabble to me, Doc."

Kara cuts into the discussion saying, "Psychobabble or not, you're going to have to get your act together right now, or I'm going to cut off every dime that you get from me. No more $10,000 designer clothes shopping sprees. No condo. No Cayenne. No nothing. You hear me?"

PD looks amazed, like Oh shit!, and he says, "Damn, Kara. That's cold! I can't believe you'd do me like that! You see what I mean, Doc? What do I have to do, Doc?"

Dr. Sullivan replies, "Well unfortunately the picture for people like you is not that bright, but I think it's worth a try. You just have to learn to keep the horse inside the corral, so to speak. In other words, if you can learn to be a liar, cheater, manipulator, and con man, you can unlearn it. Right? Now, you're just playing games."

PD thinks, *Little does he know. He's right on target with all that shit, but that's a choice, my choice.* Kara speaks up, "What you call love is conditional, PD. You only 'love' people for what you can get out of them." Dr. Sullivan pitches in and says, "Conditional love? You don't even love yourself! Not really!"

PD stands to his feet in anger, "Con man, liar, and cheat, huh?" PD's fists are balled up, eyes glaring. Dr. Sullivan raises his voice as he says in a commanding way, "Sit down. Sit down! Sit down before I kick your ass, PD!" Then Dr. Sullivan stands.

PD thinks, *Uh Oh. I guess this dude means business. I better sit my ass down.* PD is shocked as he sits down, slowly. Dr. Sullivan is embarrassed as he says, "My apology, Kara. My apology, PD. That was totally unprofessional on my part. That's not the real me. It's really not. I know I lost my cool for a minute. I can assure you that will never happen again.

Anyway, . . . PD, do you love yourself?" PD eyes the doctor as he thinks, *Well, I might as well tell the truth this time. It couldn't hurt.* PD replies, "Probably not. Hell no! My whole life, I've never had my head in a place where I could believe that anyone could love me." PD breaks down in tears, "Let's face it. I'm unlovable. You're exactly correct. That's how I grew up, knowing I'm not shit on the inside. I'm in love with that fake face that I show the world, trying to make myself look good so I can feel like a real person inside. I never felt love from a damn soul in my family or anywhere else."

PD starts sobbing profusely. Dr. Sullivan tells him, "Look at me, PD." PD looks at Dr. Sullivan with tears running down his face and they embrace. Dr. Sullivan consoles him, "Don't worry. We're going to beat this problem, together." PD thinks, *That crying shit was all an act. I think Dr. Sullivan has caught onto me though and knows that I'm going through the motions in therapy. I hate him. I hate his inner peace and most of all his ability to love, something that I know I'll never have. I hate Dr. Sullivan for every damn thing that he represents. Dr. Sullivan is dead meat! I bet he doesn't know that, but he'll find out!*

CHAPTER 15—Flashback

PD and Dr. Sullivan are working together in Dr. Sullivan's office to keep PD's thought disorder in check. PD is practicing his behavioral re-programing strategies. He is writing out homework assignments, rehearsing affirmations in the mirror, exercising, meditating, practicing positive self-talk, and listening to therapeutic recordings. Dr. Sullivan says to PD, "PD, we're going to use everything we can to help you become the decent man you say you want to become. Imagine yourself relaxing on the beach having become the respectable new PD. What's the name of your dog?" PD replies, "Killer." Dr. Sullivan says, "Breath in deeply from your stomach. Breath in, and breath out. Breath in, and breath out. Imagine that you and Killer are playing on the beach in the ocean waves. You've given up cheating, the manipulation, and the constant lies that you tell yourself." PD decides to give it a real try, no more pretending. He spent the next few months trying to meet up to what faced him if he wanted to become a respectable man. To him, this was a huge challenge, facing his inner demon. He was making progress, and then something unexpected threw him off.

PD gets called in to the police station for interrogation. In the interrogation room, Detective Cuffie and Davidson are standing and PD's mom is hidden away in the wings of the cross-examination area. PD is sitting on a chair, in a blank room with only one table and a spotlight on him. Detective Cuffie addresses PD, "Purvis Dempsey, I called you down here because we have some new evidence that you may be involved with the death of Monica Saunders." Detective Davidson pitches in, "Apparently you and she were closer than you let on before. You were the father of the baby, weren't you?" PD acts innocent and asks, "What baby?" Detective Cuffie is furious at his acting and screams, "Yours and Monica's baby, you, asshole!" PD says, "What makes you think that

Monica and I had a baby together? We were just friends."

PD's mom steps in from the alcove and speaks up, "Well, if it isn't my handsome boy." PD is surprised to see his mother at the police station, then rolls his eyes at her. PD's mom says, "Just friends? That's not what I understand, PD. You're looking kind of pale in the face. Have you been eating that confounded fried chicken again? You know it messes with your system." PD replies, "Well, just a little bit." PD's mom says, "I knew it! You know chickens urinate through their skin. No wonder you're so sickly looking."

PD replies, "Mom, chickens don't urinate through their skin. Their urine comes out with their solid waste." PD's mom doesn't listen to him. She says, "Keep on believing that bullshit, and you're going to end up impotent with premature grey hair like your Uncle Mason."

PD rolls his eyes at his mom again. PD's mom notices the eye-rolling and says, "Roll your eyes at me again, and that will be the last time you disrespect me, my handsome boy." PD finally asks, "Mom. What in the hell are you doing here anyway? I saw dad. He's an alcoholic and a crack addict, I guess. He put me out of like a hole in the wall. You're right he doesn't give a shit about me. Who would have thought? My dysfunctional family doesn't love me, not even a little bit!"

PD's mom haughtily replies, "Serves you right!" PD repeats his question, "What are you doing here?" PD's mom replies, "I'm just making sure that my sorry, irresponsible son faces the consequences of mistreating that poor, innocent girl, Monica. You murdered that poor girl, didn't you, Purvis?" Baffled, PD asks, "You told them that?" PD's mom shrugs and replies, "Why not? Did you know that Monica and the detective here were related? He was her godfather."

PD asks, "Is everybody in this damn place related?" PD's mom continues, "Then you destroyed that girl's life. That's what you always do in one way or another, male or female, destroy people's lives. You're just like your father. You destroy other people's happiness just for the thrill of it. Then you blame people for your crap. You're evil!"

PD looks disgusted as he asks, "Mom?" Detective Cuffie interrupts the family drama, "That has nothing to do with it. Fact is that we're going to have to hold you, Mr. Dempsey, until we get some loose ends tied up. Detective Davidson, escort Mr. Dempsey to lock-up." PD panics, "What? You can't do that!" Detective Cuffie replies, "Watch me!" PD struggles essentially in detective Davidson's hands as he shouts, "Mom! You turned on me!" PD's mom simply replies, "You turned on yourself. You weasel!"

PD is locked up with hardened criminals. They are staring at him like he's fresh meat for their sexual pleasure. PD is looking around, highly uncomfortable, petrified in the holding cell. The next morning PD is lost in his thoughts, *This was one of the most terrifying moments in my life. The smell in lock-up was rank beyond imagination. I was okay until they noticed me. Something about me said I was an easy target. They raped me, all night long. It felt, I can imagine, like someone had stuck a turkey carving knife up my ass and turned it on. Those nightmares of abuse from what Uncle Mason and my brother, Martin did to me came flooding back. I totally lost it! The world was against me, and I wasn't going to take it without fighting back!*

PD requests a call and decides to call Kara. As Kara picks up PD says, "Kara, did you put my mother up to ratting on me. They locked me up and raped me in jail! You finally did it, didn't you? You turned everyone against me, including my mom." PD sniffles. Kara asks in confusion, "What do you mean? I barely know your mother." PD doesn't listen to her. He says, "Well, she knows you and Monica. In fact, you are going to have to pay for what you did to me, Kara. I'm going to make you and Dr. Sullivan pay. You better watch your back. Kara is still confused as she asks, "Who's Monica?" PD hangs up on Kara.

CHAPTER 16—Hoovering

Kara is in Dr. Sullivan's office for her routine therapy session. Dr. Sullivan says, "Kara, do you understand what I'm telling you? PD could hurt you!" Kara worried. She says, "I just talked to him on the phone, and he's a basket case. He's been implicated in a murder, and they locked him up. He said they raped him in jail. He's totally falling apart, Dr. Sullivan. I think he knows that I'm here."

Dr. Sullivan replies, "I wonder how he knew that? I would venture to say that he's losing touch with reality and thinks he's God. No doubt he's paranoid too." Kara says, "My friends tell me he's running a smear campaign against me. He thinks I'm telling everyone he's bisexual, impotent, or whatever. It's all crazy and mixed up."

Dr. Sullivan tells Kara, "Don't worry. I think that you should stay with some friends until this is all over." Kara says, "I'm just puzzled. . . He knows my every move. It's almost like he's stalking me. I'm so scared!" Dr. Sullivan tells Kara, "If it would make you feel any better, I'll walk you downstairs." Dr. Sullivan walks Kara downstairs and out of the front entrance to the building. PD is standing diagonally across the street at a tourist restaurant site, after getting out of the jail because of there was no solid evidence to hold him in any more. He came there to fulfill his promise that he made to Kara on the phone.

PD thinks to himself, *So there's Dr. Sullivan—in the flesh. I know he's going to be wrapping it up at his office soon. He has to . . . It's getting late.* After a while, Dr. Sullivan exits the building and PD catches up with him. PD is carrying a brown leather man bag with all of his essential "protective" paraphilia in it. He walks up to Dr. Sullivan's side and in a creepy immature voice says, "Good evening, Doc." Dr. Sullivan asks, "What are you doing here?" PD thrusts the hand gun hard into Dr. Sullivan's rib. PD smiles and says, "I'm taking a stroll. You're coming with me. If you want to live, come stroll with me right now! You faggot bitch!" Horrified, Dr. Sullivan says,

139

"Faggot bitch? . . . Okay! . . . I'm coming." PD says, "Now, motherfucker!" PD walks Dr. Sullivan to a public parking lot not far from Dr. Sullivan's office and pushes him into the Cayenne.

PD commands him, "Get in the car, you pussy! Lay back. I have something for you." PD pulls out a pair of handcuffs, lays Dr. Sullivan's seat all the way back in a reclining position, duct tapes his head to the head rest, duct tapes his torso to the chair, and cuffs his hands. PD makes a menacing smile; stating, "Oh yes, since we don't really know each other very well, may I have a business card? I was thinking about making a referral."

Dr. Sullivan replies in a shaky voice, "Okay! I think I have a few business cards inside of my sport coat jacket pocket, PD. Take it! Just don't hurt me! You don't have to do this!" PD replies with a cunning lunacy, "They always say that! You didn't have to team up with my bitch, Kara, and try to destroy my career." Dr. Sullivan asks in confusion and panic, "What the hell? What are you talking about? I'm not teaming up with anybody!"

PD replies, "You, lying, motherfucking turd. You said that I don't have any balls. I heard you on my listening device. You thought your sessions were totally private. Didn't you?" Then PD says in a childlike voice, "You're not my friend!" He changes characters and talks in his normal voice, "You said that you were going to help me fight the odds. Now, you're against me, bitch."

Using a syringe, PD injects Dr. Sullivan in the neck with a slow-acting sedative, and Dr. Sullivan is very slowly losing consciousness. PD look askance as he says, "Well, I'll show you balls!" PD drives Dr. Sullivan to an isolated, secluded, newly, constructed public park where no one can see what he is doing to Dr. Sullivan. PD says, "Let's pull down these pants of yours. That'll be cute!" The whole car is rocking back and forth as he attacks the doctor.

Dr. Sullivan screams for help, "Oh, no! . . . Please. . . Don't! . . . Help!"

Semiconscious, Dr. Sullivan faints. After completing his handiwork, PD soaks the Cayenne with gasoline, sets it on fire, and leaves the crime scene carrying a small box and a large brown valise. He walks several blocks away from the park, and summons an Uber on his phone to take him home. The Uber driver arrives and the driver asks PD, "Do you smell that? What is that smell, like something burning?" PD says, "It's probably some asshole playing with matters that he never should have gotten involved with in the first place. The driver says, "What? What do you mean?" PD: "Oh, nothing. Let's get moving." They begin the ride to PD's apartment. PD enters his apartment and snorts cocaine as he laughs and then makes a cold, heartless, stone-faced expression and stares off into space.

Kara returns to her apartment. She's drinking a cocktail. As she walks from her dining room to the loft entertainment area, the doorbell rings. She sees that its PD at the door. Clearly mystified and alarmed Kara asks, "One second. What are you doing here? How did you get in here? This is supposed to be a secure building."

PD has a wild look in his eyes and dawns a five o'clock scruffy beard. The cocaine makes him sniffle a lot. PD is more disheveled than usual and loosely aligned with reality. He retorts, "My friend, the doorman, let me up. I have a duplicate of your elevator key. Don't ask me how I got it." He barges past her into the apartment, holding a small gift-wrapped box behind him and another large locking leather valise but in black, unlike the valise that he was carrying before. Kara asks gingerly, "What do you want?" PD smirks and says, "I want you to get what you deserve! I brought you something, a little gift! Well, two little gifts."

He sets the large black valise off to the side of the entrance to the apartment while directing Kara's attention to the gift box. Kara opens the gift-wrapped box, with a bow on top. Kara has a visual flashback to Dr. Sullivan's warning during the therapy session with

Dr. Sullivan, "He may be dangerous. He's a narcopath!" Kara thinks, *He is really losing it. It could happen at any time.*

PD continues, "It's from Dr. Sullivan, in the flesh. Don't you want to see the beautiful present I brought you from him?" Kara eyes the gift box as she replies in a trembling voice, "Okay, let's open it." She tears off the wrapping. Inside of the box is Dr. Sullivan's business card. Also, inside of the box are two fleshy-looking objects covered with blood. Kara can't believe it. Kara feels nauseated as she asks, "Is this what I think it is?" PD says in an almost excited tone, "What do you think it is? It's just like one of those 1970s godfather, gangster movies, a couple of nuts, you know, balls, testicles, gift-wrapped in a box! How original? Now I guess we can see who doesn't have any balls, corny huh? Dr. Sullivan's! Look in the box!"

Kara screams in terror, "You're sick, PD!" PD asks, "What are you screaming about?" Kara's heart is beating fast as she asks a question she already knows the answer to, "Are you insane?" PD replies, "You mean am I a narcissistic psycho like Dr. Sullivan said when I was listening in your therapy session?" Kara says, "Listening in? How? You listened to my therapy session?" PD goes on, "I listened to your fucking therapy session. So what!" PD mocks Dr. Sullivan. Some people say, "Yes. I'm a psycho . . . " Then he shrugs his shoulders and says malevolently, " . . . but I don't give a fuck!"

Kara asks in shock, "Don't you have any loyalty?" PD simply replies, "Yes! I do! My loyalty, my allegiance is solely to PD, Purvis Dempsey. I deserve it! Dr. Sullivan called my image of myself a fantasy, and yes, I love that part of me and so do you!"

Kara says, "PD, be reasonable. I can help you." PD asks, "Help me? You have been trying to destroy me the whole time. Susan told me so! Susan never lies!" Kara is slowly backing into the kitchen, looking for something to use as a weapon to protect herself. PD continues, "Dr. Sullivan doesn't know everything. He says that I'm going insane and that I have a rotten heart. Anyway, you'd be surprised how well you can hear those private conversations with the right listening gear, the amulet. I use my cell phone to listen in, you bitch. It even tracks your calendar, Kara." He laughs and says, "You fuckin' fool! Well, it's time you learned a lesson."

PD lunges at Kara. She picks up a hammer that the handyman who had been working in the apartment left for her. Kara takes the hammer off the counter and swings it at him barely grazing him across his forehead. PD says, "Oh!!!!!! That hurt! I'm going to fucking kill you, Kara!" Kara runs into her bedroom and locks the door behind her. PD tries to break down the door by kicking and using his shoulder to break open the door, once, twice, three times, but to no avail.

Kara shouts, "When even your own mom says you're an asshole, there must be something to it. You're an asshole, you motherfucker! You proved it." In a narcissistic rage, PD is not bothered by her taunts and replies, "Yeah. You're so complimentary. I'm going to kill you, bitch! Yes, because I'm an asshole!"

In anger, PD pushes hard with his shoulder against the door. PD continues, "I heard you telling Dr. Sullivan how you were going to tell everyone on me." Kara says, "You've got it confused. It's more like the reverse, PD. I know that you've been bad-mouthing me to everyone you run across." PD replies in a soft and child-like manner, "I don't hurt people!" Kara says, "I know everyone worth knowing in this town! You think I'm stupid? What you say I'm doing to you, you're actually trying to do to me. PD, you need help! You really need fucking help!" PD shouts, "No, you need help, Kara! You need a hell lot of a help, right about now!" PD pounds hard against the door. Kara screams, "Get away from that door!" PD threatens her, "Bitch, I'm going to tell you one more time. Open this fucking door!" Kara says, "I'm going to do what I have to do, PD."

Kara pulls out a pistol from her nightstand. She keeps it there just for an occasion like this, and shoots several bullets through the door above PD's head. Then she shouts, "Get your ass out of here!" PD runs out of the apartment as fast as he can. Kara thinks, *He ought to be glad I didn't shoot his ass.* She falls to her knees on the floor and breaks down in tears. Kara says out loud to herself, "I love you, PD! I love you so much why don't you understand!"

Kara pulls herself together and thinks, *I should have seen the signs. You never really know what you've got until you get a chance to peel back the mask. PD, you're not going to shit on me anymore! Never! No matter what!*

CHAPTER 17—Boom

Kara is totally shaken up from PD's visit, when she hears her phone ring. She picks up, "Ms. Taylor, Ms. Kara Taylor? This is Detective Anthony Cuffie with the police department." Kara makes a sigh of relief, as she replies, "Yes. This is she. Thank God! I was just getting ready to call the police. I need your help!" Detective Cuffie replies, "Oh really? From looking at the appointment schedule, I understand that you were one of Dr. Albert Sullivan's clients, and you had an appointment with him one evening, recently." Kara responds, "Yes. Correct." Detective Cuffie continues, "I hate to tell you this, but they found Dr. Sullivan's dead body at a park, you know the old rock quarry. It's under construction. He'd been tortured, and the weirdest part of it was that his testicles were taken. Can you tell me anything about this?" Kara replies in shock, "Oh my God! No! I know it can't be true! It can't be. I just saw him, and he warned me. What am I going to do?" Detective Cuffie asks in confusion, "Warned you about what?" Kara replies, "Sorry, Detective Cuffie. I'm really shaken up and not thinking straight. If you only knew what I just went through. I'll tell you what I know, but I'm really scared. I'll talk to you face-to-face but not on the phone!" Detective Cuffie says, "I'll be over your place in less than an hour. What's your address?" Kara replies, "I'll text it to you on this number. Come as soon as possible!"

Shortly after escaping from Kara's apartment, PD calls Kara on her cell phone. Kara notices the leather bag that PD left, answers the call, and says, "What are you doing calling me again, PD?" PD talks mean to her. He says, "You tried to kill me . . . ." Kara cuts him off, ". . . If I wanted to kill you, I would have shot through the door; not above your head, stupid!" PD replies yelling loudly like a spoiled child, "You're not my friend!" When Kara hears PD say this, she re-experiences a flashback of one of the therapy sessions with Dr. Sullivan and what he said about PD. *Dr. Sullivan says, I think he's starting to lose touch with reality. He's emotionally like a dangerous four-year old, a four-year old in a man's body. He's deadly.*

PD brings her back to reality as he says in a tearful, child-like voice, "You're not my friend! I'm going to kill you, you, asshole! . . . Booooom!" PD is trying to intimidate her. Kara says, "What . . . ?" Something in her gut told Kara to look in that leather bag that PD left near her front door, and she sees what looks like a bomb." Petrified for a second or two, Kara is absolutely shocked, but she plays it smart and keeps him on the phone long enough to escape. She makes a mad rush out of her apartment.

Shortly afterwards, we see that PD is standing across from Kara's apartment building as he hangs up and waits for a few minutes to start some fun, not realizing that Kara had already discovered the bomb. He pushes the detonator. A massive explosion takes out much of the sixth floor, but Kara manages to run out of the back door of the apartment building. The explosion knocks her face forward to the ground. PD smiles like a mad man and thinks, *It's all her fault! Poor thing! She forgot to remove the black leather bag in her apartment, the bomb. Boom!!!!*

PD suddenly experiences a series of flashbacks from different times over many years when he was growing. *PD's mom says, "I wish I never had you. Every time I look at you, I see your drunk-ass father. Even his sorry girlfriend that he cheated with on me wouldn't put up with his pitiful ass. It broke my heart! She put his alcoholic crack head out! I hate you, PD. I never loved you because of him, your dad. You're just like him. I should have aborted you. You make me want to puke! You're going to stay with Uncle Mason."*

In this flashback, PD is nine years old, crying and whimpering, lying curled up on his side in a fetal position having been assaulted. PD is locked in the closet for days at a time, especially when his "guardian", Uncle Mason, is binge drinking on the weekend. Uncle Mason says, "I don't know why you're crying like a little girl. That's why I can't stand your ass! You're such a little faggot! Didn't I tell you you're going to have to sell that ass? I have to pay the rent this month, boy! You got a lot of customers who want to see your pretty little ass! Maybe if you do good you can have some ice cream, later.

Young PD asks with a twinkle in his eyes, "Ice cream? Yes, Sir."
Uncle Mason says in an evil tone, "Speaking of that, get over here, and get to work!" Mason molests PD mercilessly.

CHAPTER 18—Walking Contradiction

PD snorts two lines of cocaine. High as a kite, he walks down the midtown boulevard in the late afternoon, carrying another brown valise this time. Fading in and out of a delusional state, PD talks to himself, "I'm going to pay back every fuckin' bastard who hurt me. I mean *everybody* is going to have to pay!" PD pulls out of the brown valise, the automatic pistol. He begins to shoot 5, 10, and then 15 random pedestrians, periodically re-loading. Some people are in cars and one car's driver runs into a fire hydrant causing a 20-foot vertical gusher of water. PD's eyes lock on an eight- or nine-year old little boy. The little boy is frozen with fear and cannot move.

The little boy asks in a frightened shaky voice, "Are you going to shoot me too, mister?" PD replies in a child-like manner as he's mentally disturbed, "I don't hurt people."

Not far away, in route to Kara's apartment, Detective Cuffie hears the gun fire and rushes to the scene. Detective Cuffie sees the horrid scene of multiple bodies in front of him and immediately alerts the police station on the radio, "Shots fired. I think we've got a mass shooting in progress. We have multiple citizens down and an officer. Get some back up here! Now!" In the midst of the chaos, PD is able to escape into the park. The police lose him and no one can describe him well enough to track him down. In the park bathroom, he takes a shirt out of the brown man bag and puts it over the shirt that he is wearing. He puts on a hat and a bandanna around his neck. PD ditches the bag and the weapon in a trash bin. He circles back around to the scene of the shooting to appear to help the shooting victims. He approaches several shooting victims. None of them recognize him because of the disguise, except for the little boy.

After pretending to help the shooting victims, PD walks toward an abandoned building where the little boy is standing. PD says in a whisper, "Don't

worry. I'm here to help. I don't hurt people. I help!"
The little boy says in an innocent voice, "Help people?
Thanks for not shooting me, mister."

PD asks in confusion, "How did you know it was me?"
The little boy answers, "Your eyes! They're like a
fawn's eyes, a baby deer. Anyway, I could tell from
your heart. You're just like me inside, but you
shouldn't hurt people." PD takes a moment to digest
what the little boy said and then replies, "I don't want
to hurt you, boy." The little boy watches PD run into
the abandoned building. PD enters the clandestine
building where he's been many times before living out
his drug-induced, delusional alternate reality. He uses
this hideaway whenever he is in a funk, distressed or
depressed. He uses a key to unlock the door. This is
his make-shift place of refuge and "worship" for him.
He puts on a priest-like robe and begins to chant.

PD chants like he's in some kind of trance, "I
can do what I want; when I want, as long as I forgive
myself. I'm God. I can do what I want; when I want, as
long as I forgive myself. I'm God. I can do what I

want; when I want, as long as I forgive myself. I'm God." Shortly afterwards, Detective Cuffie enters the building since in his haste PD leaves the building door wide open. Detective Cuffie shouts, "Young man! Raise your hands. You're going to have to come with me!" Staring his big eyes at the officer, PD asks, "Why do you want me to go with you?" Detective Cuffie replies, "You shot all of those people, huh? I talked to a little boy outside. He saw you run in here. So, who else would it be but you in here? You spared his life. Why did you do that—spare his life?" PD answers in a drab voice, "He reminded me of myself when I was nine. That's why I didn't shoot him. Not like the others." Detective Cuffie asks, "What about the others?" PD contorts his face in anger as he replies, "They raped me over and over and over again. They beat me. Made me sleep in the closet for days. Gave me ice cream when I was good. I got away. I'm God. They raped me again, just last week after you put me in jail. My own mother betrayed me. Did you think about that Sir? Do you have any ice cream?"

Detective Cuffie answers closely watching PD's every move, "I'm afraid not." PD asks, "Can you help me? I can't do this anymore!" Detective Cuffie asks, "Do what?" PD's lower lip trembles as he replies, "Be a faggot bitch." PD falls apart, emotionally a basket case, crying uncontrollably. He decompensates and continues with his chant, "I can do what I want when I want, as long as I forgive myself. I'm God. I can do what I want when I want, as long as I forgive myself. I'm God."

As he is repeating this hypnotic phrase, PD picks up the sharp hunting knife off the make-shift alter from behind him where Detective Cuffie cannot see it. He attempts to cut his throat. Detective Cuffie swiftly moves into action toward him in an attempt to save his life. Detective Cuffie tackles PD, wrestling him to the ground. They struggle, but PD is too weak compared to the detective. Detective Cuffie takes the knife from PD and handcuffs him. Detective Cuffie pulls him up as he says, "Come on. Let's go, my friend." As if in a fog, PD asks, "Go where?" Detective

Cuffie replies, "Somewhere where you will be safe."
PD is still repeating his trance-like chant as he is
bleeding a little from his neck from the knife wound.

CHAPTER 19—Doodles for Old Times Sake

Staff and patients are busy walking back and forth on the psychiatric ward. A patient is repeatedly screaming at the top of her lungs, "I want a man!", from the seclusion room. Psychiatric nurse, "Yes, may I help you? What's your name, sir?" Uncle Mason replies, "Mason Dempsey. I'm Purvis Dempsey's uncle. We call him "PD". I haven't seen him for over twenty years. Is there any way that I could see him?" The psychiatric nurse asks, "ID?" Uncle Mason shows his ID. After checking some documents, the psychiatric nurse says, "I believe you are listed in the file as the next of kin or an emergency contact, except for his brother, Martin. Purvis attempted suicide." Uncle Mason asks in disbelief, "Attempted suicide?" The psychiatric nurse informs Uncle Mason, "He tried to cut his throat with a hunting knife. The detective saved his life." Uncle Mason says, "Wow! Just between me and you, he's been through a lot of serious situations in his life, a lot of trauma and abuse, they say. Is there any way that I can see him?" The psychiatric nurse replies, "That should be fine, but remember that he's barely hanging on by a thread, emotionally. He's on suicide watch. He probably needs some outside, healthy stimulation. Let me show you where he is."

The nurse walks Uncle Mason to the seclusion room where PD is lying on the bed on his side wearing hospital pajamas in his classic fetal position, this time sucking his thumb. The nurse tells Uncle Mason, "Here he is" and returns to the nurse's station. Uncle Mason asks, "PD, is that you?"

PD sniffles as he repeats his chant almost perpetually, "I can do what I want; when I want, as long as I forgive myself. I'm God. I can do what I want; when I want, as long as I forgive myself. I'm God. I can do what I want; when I want, as long as I forgive myself. I'm God." Uncle Mason asks, "PD, is that you? It's Uncle Mason." PD is barely perceptible in his reply at first, "Uncle who? Uncle Mason? Uncle Mason. It's been a long time since I've seen you.

Please, ask the nurse if we can spend some time in the
day room together; so, we can talk like we used to. Ask
her for a couple of sharp pencils and paper so we can
doodle. Please?"

Uncle Mason simply says, "Okay. Hold on!" as
he goes to the nurse's station to ask permission for
him and PD to sit in the day room where they can talk
and doodle. Uncle Mason returns from the nurse's
station with the nurse. The nurse opens the door and
lets Uncle Mason and PD proceed to the day room.
Uncle Mason and PD sit down in the day room to talk.
PD doodles on a note pad using the paper and a
couple of pencils. Uncle Mason converses with PD
saying, "Yeah, I figure I owe it to you to come see you.
It's been a long time."

PD sniffles again and he replies slightly
agitated, "Owe it to me? Owe it to me?" Uncle Mason
picks up a package and offers it to PD stating, "I
brought you some ice cream." PD stares at Uncle
Mason with big doe-like eyes and asks, "Ice cream?"
As he hears about the ice cream, he slips into a trance,

having a flashback in his mind and imagining himself at age nine. PD sees Uncle Mason sexually assaulting him in exchange for ice cream and he breaks into tears. PD says, "Uncle Mason. I remember now, clearly.   You hurt me! You hurt me really bad, and you did it over and over and over, selling me to those perverts. You abused me for a long, long time, not just once! How could you do that to me? I was just a kid. You molested me, sexually and treated me like your little bitch. You're a fucking criminal. You just never got caught!"

Uncle Mason replies, "How was I supposed to take care of you? You weren't even my kid. I couldn't work after that serious car accident I was in. You remember that? I tried to pay the rent, keep the lights on, and buy food. I tried hard—"

PD cuts his sentence off, ". . . So you decided to take advantage of me, huh? I was a kid, and you pimped me to a bunch of perverts. You treated me like your little bitch. You sold me for rent money. Age nine of all things! How could I defend myself? That's a low down, dirty, motherfucking trick!"

Uncle Mason rolls his eyes and scorns PD, "Anyway, you wanted it, just like you wanted that ice cream! Don't try to blame me because you liked to lick those guy's balls or whatever at age nine." Disgusted, PD asks, "Liked it? You know what you call that? You're a fucking pedophile yourself, but you're the worst kind, one who preys on his own family. You're sick! That's incest, you fucking bastard."

Mason answers with contempt, "It would only be incest if your little sissy ass didn't want it so bad. You ought to be glad anybody took you in and took care of your sorry ass. Faggot bitch!" PD's eyes immediately well up, and he breaks into a flood of tears. He sees Uncle Mason's face during the abusive incidents and remembers what Uncle Mason used to call him during the abusive episodes. He said, *PD, you faggot bitch!*

He completely loses it. Furious and irate, PD scowls at Mason in a fit of rage and yells, "Bullshit! . . .

Bullshit, bullshit, bullshit! You son of a bitch! You dirty, trifling son of a bitch!" PD springs to his feet across the day room table and stabs Mason in the jugular with one of the pencils and with the other pencil he stabs him in his left eye, straight into the middle of Mason's head. Mason dies instantly while the blood pours out of his body everywhere in the day room. PD stands up with both arms spread to his left and right as he mumbles his trance-like chant. The other patients panic at the horrid scene and several nurses run towards PD to inject him with a sedative in order to keep him in control.

CHAPTER 20—Escape to Fantasy Land

PD lies curled up on his side in a fetal position sucking his thumb, completely out of touch with reality in a semi-catatonic state. The attendant comes to the door and slips the tray of food through the seclusion room door. The hospital attendant closely observes PD as he asks, "Hey, PD. Are you feeling any better now? Maybe you should eat something. We've got some great lasagna for you today. If you're really good, then you can have some ice cream!"

Spoken as a thought inside PD's head, he hears, *Faggot bitch!* Suddenly PD opens his eyes as if in a state of shock and says to himself, "I'm not going out like this. I refuse. I deserve better. Dr. Sullivan was right!" He remembers what the doctor said to him. *Dr. Sullivan, "You have to embrace your healing deep in your soul as if you are already the new Purvis Dempsey, the re-designed PD."* PD imagines, *I am lying on a divine, beautiful, white, sandy beach thinking about my life-long ordeal and the struggle to overcome my mental nightmare. I'm laughing and playing in the ocean waves with my French Bulldog, "Killer" It took years to get a handle on my demon and to tame the horse. All that I needed to do is keep it inside of the corral, as Dr. Sullivan would say.*

If I could learn to take advantage of people, then I could unlearn it. I remember the lessons he taught me. Thanks to him, I can lead a calm life. Suddenly his positive train of thoughts transforms into detrimental thoughts. *It's sad that Dr. Sullivan had to die. He deserved it. Some secrets are best taken to the grave. I'm one of the few people ever to overcome this, whatever this is. The 25th demon reigns no more.* PD starts giggling uncontrollably.

PD is lying on his cot mumbling to himself as Detective Cuffie, the ward psychiatrist, and Kara are conversing in the hallway. Detective Cuffie greets the doctor and says, "Hey Doctor. I guess you know that your patient has been implicated in a number of very, very mysterious deaths in the area. That's not to mention the murder of his uncle in the hospital day room. Oh, by the way, this is Kara Taylor. The ward psychiatrist smiles as he replies, "Hello, Kara. I know you've been through a lot. Is there anything I can do for you?" Kara answers, "Oh, no. Thanks."

Detective Cuffie continues, "The problem is that we haven't been able to link him to many of the deaths. I do think he killed my goddaughter, Monica. We don't really have any hard evidence, a button from his jacket isn't enough, except for the death of his uncle in the day room whose name is Mason Dempsey." Kara joins in, "He also tried to kill me." The ward psychiatrist asks, "What are you going to do with yourself now, Kara?" Kara sighs as she replies, "Help other abuse survivors heal." The psychiatrist nods as he says, "Well, the one thing that we can be sure about is that it'll be a couple of lifetimes before he gets out of any psychiatric institution, like this one. Fundamentally, he meets the legal definition for insanity: Danger to self and others."

Smiling, Kara walks out to the psychiatry ward elevator. Her smile turns into a tear as she gazes up to the elevator ceiling and the elevator door closes. Detective Cuffie sees her go and decides to catch up with her to see if she's okay, "Have a good evening, Doctor."

Night silence fills PD's hospital room for several minutes. He hears the loud rhythmic sound of his heart beating as he goes into a semiconscious state. In his mind, he sees a high-speed series of horrifying scenes of people whom he has worked tirelessly to tame and destroy. He is callously unaffected as a sick smirk washes across PD's face and his eyes open widely as he says in a whisper, "I don't hurt people! Hurt people hurt me!"

THE END

Narcissistic Emotional Abuse Techniques Glossary

The following are techniques that a narcissist like PD may use. Where in The 25th Demon do you see the characters using these manipulation and control methods? What traits do you see the characters using?

Withholding–Withholding love, affection, empathy, and intimacy Countering – This is when the partner expresses a thought and the abuser immediately counters that view with his/her own without really listening to or considering it.

Discounting–When the abuser discounts the partner's views or thoughts, tells the partner those ideas are insignificant, incorrect, or stupid. The abuser may even discount the partner's memory about the abuse itself.

Blocking and diverting–When the partner wants to discuss a concern, the abuser changes the subject and prevents any discussion and resolution.

Accusing and blaming–The abuser will accuse the partner of some offense. The abuser may well know the partner is innocent of the supposed offense, but this tactic serves the purpose of putting the partner on the defensive rather than seeing clearly the behavior of the abuser.

Judging and criticizing–This serves to weaken the partner's self-esteem and increases their looking to the abuser for validation.

Trivializing–This is when the abuser minimizes something that is important to the partner, such as a concern about something the abuser has done.

Undermining–When the partner wants to do something positive in her/his life, the abuser becomes threatened and tries to stop the partner. It may be an overt command, or it may be trying to subtly convince the partner why it's a bad idea.

Threatening–This can include threats of divorce, of leaving, of abuse, or other threats of actions that would hurt (not necessarily physically) the partner or someone the partner cares about.

 Forgetting–This includes the abuser 'forgetting' about incidents of abuse, which undermines the partner's reality. The abuser may also 'forget' about things that they know are very important to their partner.

Ordering–Treating the partner as a child or a slave; denying the independence of the partner.

Denial–Similar to discounting, although here the abuser outright denies his/her
actions. This discounts the reality of a partner.

Abusive Anger–When the abuser becomes enraged to the point of frightening the partner. This rage often is caused by incidents that a non-abuser would consider insignificant.

Reference
http://thenarcissisticlife.com/the-narcissist-and-emotional-abuse/

Other survivor community terms:

Cold shoulder—Ignoring the survivor as a method of manipulation; usually so that the survivor will seek to regain the initial relationship between the narcissist and survivor when they were initially "happy" during "lovebombing". (The survivor finds out that the narcissist use lovebombing to reel the survivor in for later manipulation and control.)

Devaluation—The narcissist demeans and devalues the target individual; especially once the person is no longer a challenge or unwilling to boost the narcissist's ego.

Discard—The narcissist separates from the survivor without conscience or any form of attachment. The narcissist does not love or miss people and never looks back because they never cared about the survivor in the first place.

Gaslighting—Distorting facts, situations, and events to make a person question the person's judgment.

Grand finale—The narcissist breaks off the relationship in a tremendously dramatic final production.

Going grey rock—Ignoring the narcissist and refusing to react to manipulation for the positive or negative response that the narcissist is seeking.

Flying monkeys—People who knowingly or unknowingly do the narcissist's bidding resulting from manipulation and trickery.

Hoovering—After disconnecting with the abuse survivor for a period, returning to reconnect and regain the rush that the narcissist gets from abusing the survivor.

Narcissistic rage—The narcissist goes into a frenzied fit of anger reportedly, by some survivors, at times accompanied by a terrifying facial expression that looks hellishly demonic.

Lovebombing—Overwhelming the target person for later emotional abuse by providing constant attention and gratification.

Trauma bond—The difficult-to-break link between the narcissist and survivor resulting from the warm to cold cycle of kindness and abuse that the survivor experiences from the narcissist. (Also known as a soul tie in the faith community and Stockholm Syndrome in the scientific community.)

Narcissist Diagnostic Traits

A pervasive pattern of grandiosity (in fantasy or behavior), need for admiration, and lack of empathy, beginning by early adulthood and present in a variety of contexts, as indicated by five (or more) of the following:

1. Has a grandiose sense of self-importance (e.g., exaggerates achievements and talents, expects to be recognized as superior without commensurate achievements)
2. Is preoccupied with fantasies of unlimited success, power, brilliance, beauty, or ideal love
3. Believes that he or she is "special" and unique and can only be understood by, or should associate with, other special or high-status people (or institutions)
4. Requires excessive admiration
5. Has a sense of entitlement, i.e., unreasonable expectations of especially favorable treatment

or automatic compliance with his or her expectations
6. Is interpersonally exploitative, i.e., takes advantage of others to achieve his or her own ends
7. Lacks empathy: is unwilling to recognize or identify with the feelings and needs of others
8. Is often envious of others or believes that others are envious of him or her
9. Shows arrogant, haughty behaviors or attitudes

Ways to Protect Yourself from Narcissistic Abuse

Pay attention to gut-level feelings. If something about the person feels wrong, then it probably is wrong. Don't try to explain it away.

See if the person looks down on others; especially restaurant help, for example.

Avoid getting into serious relationships. If the person is a narcissist, it is only a matter of time before the mask comes off and they reveal themselves through their self-centered behavior.

Pay attention to putdowns and micro-insults; especially early in the relationship. Avoid explaining them away.

If you find yourself researching what is wrong with the relationship by looking on the Internet and other sources, there is probably something wrong with the relationship. You may be dealing with a narcissist.

A long string of broken relationships on the part of the person is a red flag that he or she could be a narcissist.

If the person seems to always be on the cell phone and conveniently unavailable on a consistent basis, they may be searching out new sources to be manipulated and controlled.

Hypersensitivity to feedback and criticism is often another characteristic of a narcissist. They may find it difficult to handle disagreement since everything that they believe is true is the gospel.

Everything they say is right, and everything you say is wrong. You may find yourself walking on egg shells.

They get irritated about small items or events that most people would ignore. As a result, they have adult temper tantrums for seemingly no reason.

They compulsively lie about large and small things; many of which don't matter to the average person and the narcissist would be better off telling the truth.

Easily bored and constantly restless with little follow-through on much of anything. Jumps from one project to the next often.

Avoid sharing any personal information with the narcissist since they often remember every minute detail of anything that they can use as a weapon later.

Remember! Everyone is not a narcissist. Some people are simply bad actors. Avoid going overboard with diagnosing people.

Listen to experienced survivors and go not contact with the narcissist whenever possible. That means no texts, phone calls, emails, personal interactions, etc. unless absolutely necessary. (Consider yourself very fortunate never to have a relationship with the narcissist again.)

Printed in Great Britain
by Amazon